To Val

RUBY SLIPS
AND POKER CHIPS

HEATHER M KINDT

Heath Kindt

Moyhill Publishing

Printing History
Kindle Edition 2017.
EPUB Edition 2017.

Editing by Dan Alatorre.
Book Layout by *Moyhill* Publishing.

Dedication

*To my husband Tom, who believed in me
even when I didn't believe in myself.*

Contents

Chapter 1

A tornado blew through the small town of Quandary the night before Westward arrived. The slim, rope-like twister was a two on the Fujita scale, but the damage it caused seemed more like a five. I wondered later if the storm came to drop her off before moving further east. The very next day, the school board voted and named Maxine Westward the new principal of Quandary Elementary. That day changed my life.

Now you may be wondering what I have against a woman who gives her life to shaping young minds. It just so happens that I was born with a sixth sense called woman's intuition. When Maxine first walked into the school for her interview with her briefcase and painted-on smile, it was easy to size her up.

As I raced around the corner to copy my students' homework in the last minute of music class, Maxine and I nearly had a head-on collision. She wore a navy blue power suit, six-inch heels, and her hair short and red. I wondered if the state sent her to inspect the school's records again. The Kansas Department of Education has a nasty habit of sending their cronies in at the most inconvenient times.

I held up a homework sheet and extended my free hand. "I'm sorry, trying to get this done before I have to pick up the kiddos. I'm Dottie Gale."

The phony looked me up and down, frowned, and brushed past me into the office. Glancing down, I searched for the coffee stain on my satin shirt. She painted her smile on again for Miggy Samuels, the school secretary, while I made my way to the printer. Before I even knew why she was there, my intuition kicked in, telling me she was no good for my school.

"I'm here for an appointment," she said, looking around the office like she was too important to set foot in it.

I wanted to tell her to take her heels, and get back to where she came from, but instead, I bit my lip and continued my copying. I kept my ears tuned in, pretending to mind my own business. I wondered why the school board was all there, getting the royal breakfast treatment from Wanda Jo in the lunchroom. A day of interviews to find the new principal would have to start with bacon and a short stack.

⌒◡◡⌒

After school, I carried my stepladder out to the hallway to hang up my end of the school year bulletin board. The large, yellow butcher paper curled around me as I struggled to staple the first corner. One of the magazines my Uncle Embry subscribed to ran an article last year about the ten most hazardous jobs. I wanted to call the editor and give him a piece of my mind, because coal miners and structural construction workers have nothing on teachers. I could fall backwards and break my neck on the linoleum while hanging this stupid paper, not to mention the number of germs that attacked my body from the petri dishes on feet called second graders. Just as I ruined my fifth staple,

I felt a hand lift the paper. Corbin Lane stretched it across the board, holding while I attached the students' work.

"So did you hire the witch?" I watched him out of the corner of my eye. Corbin was the youngest member of the school board, as well as my ex-boyfriend. His black hair hung adorably in his eyes in a wistful fashion that reminded me of one of the characters in a comic book.

"And which one would that be, Dear?" I hated when he called me that. I slammed another staple into the wall, intent on taking my aggressions out on the bulletin board instead of Corbin.

"Which one? The red head, of course! She marches in here with her superior attitude and expects we can't see through it." I hopped down from the ladder, moving it to the center of the board. Climbing back up, I pounded my fist into the stapler, again concealing my emotions in a way that I'm sure the stapler didn't appreciate.

"We haven't made a decision, yet." He smirked. "But I guess I know where you stand." Corbin moved the ladder this time and applied the next staple.

I froze realizing my mistake. Ever since he cheated on me in high school, he was constantly trying to please me—to the point of being highly annoying.

I snatched the stapler from Corbin's hand, but found it empty. "Damn stapler."

"Here, let me take it." He took my abused weapon and went to my desk to rummage for more ammo while I thought about how I'd now become the sixth person on the interview committee. I knew my comments would definitely influence Corbin's decision. Looking back, I wished I had the sexual prowess to influence the other three men on the board. I guess I need a little more Ginger and a little less Mary Anne.

The summer came and went and I almost forgot about the impending disaster ready to take down Quandary Elementary. During the teacher workdays before school started, Westward went out of her way to impress the staff by buying doughnuts for the break room, taking us out to lunch, and sharing childhood photographs. At the end of teacher training, I was looking forward to the first day of school and the excitement of the children seeing their friends, everyone looking their best, and a chance for all of us to start over. Surveying my class, I knew I was ready to take on the school year despite the she-devil in the principal's office.

"Good morning, boys and girls. I'm Miss Gale. Please put your school supplies in your desk while I take attendance." My students worked on their desks and I collected lunch money.

Ms. Westward walked in, taking the time to frown in my direction before heading to the front of the class. "Children, I'm the new principal, Ms. Westward. I moved here from Colorado last spring. I expect that as long as I don't find you in my office, we will have a good relationship." She glanced around the classroom, her lips set in a firm line. One of the boys, knee deep in school supplies, raised his hand.

"Yes, young man?" Westward sighed and smoothed out her suit, ready to move her heels to another classroom.

"I'm Tommy." The boy wiped his nose on his sleeve. A shiny line of snot ran across his right cheek. Westward raised an eyebrow.

"Yes, Tommy." Her face was frozen into a forced smile, only interrupted by a twitch that developed in her left eye. The degrading tone made me squirm, even though it would roll off the back of a seven-year-old.

"Mr. Rollins used to play soccer at recess. Are you going to play with us?"

A slight giggle escaped my lips, and the principal's eyes looked directly at mine, shooting daggers. It was the first time that I noticed she wore contacts. Lilac? Possibly she had been a victim of a nuclear accident.

Maxine let out a long breath. "No, Tommy. Ms. Westward needs to dress in nice clothes for work, and I'm getting a little old for soccer. Maybe Miss Gale will play with you." A smile crossed her lips that told me the game was on.

"How old are you? You look like you're a hundred. That's probably why you can't play soccer."

The students erupted into laughter, while Maxine quickly left the room. I pushed my lips together to suppress a giggle of my own, but knew I had won this battle, and I would win the war with the students on my side.

Chapter 2

The month of October brought the usual things: heavier coats, autumn leaves, increased runny noses, and teacher evaluations. I welcomed the first two, but the others I could do without. At least half the staff dreaded evaluations under the new regime. With Mr. Rollins, we knew what to expect. He sat us down ahead of time with our preplanned lesson and asked us if we anticipated any snags in our plan. The day of the evaluation, he strolled in sporting his red evaluation tie. He had a tie for every special occasion. Pumpkins for Halloween, flags for Veteran's Day, hearts for Valentine's Day—and the black one for when he was fighting with his wife. Which was at least once a week according to Miggy Samuels.

Evaluation week this year began with a staff meeting held in the teacher's lounge. Being a rural school, our teacher's lounge was in the modular building near the back of the school. The last place you wanted to be during a tornado was in a trailer or modular. It was apparent to me that the school board believed their teachers expendable.

After picking up the floor to help out Mike, the school custodian, on Monday afternoon, I wandered next door to shoot the breeze with Saundie, the third grade teacher. Her fiancé traveled the country selling insurance to big corporations. It wasn't that I preferred Saundie over the other teachers, it's just that she happens to have a couch and it gave me a chance to kick off the shoes and relax for a few moments.

"So what do you think the evaluations are going to look like this year?" Saundie shoved the piles of papers on her desk into an empty drawer in her file cabinet. The art of organized illusion is one of the first skills a teacher picks up while she is student teaching. My secret stash resides in the cabinet under my sink.

"I can't imagine it'll be anything but trouble." I blew my bangs off my forehead in frustration and glanced at the clock. Almost half past three. Rollins never started the staff meetings at the designated time. Once all the teachers were there, we discussed students, an upcoming snowstorm, or who was coming to happy hour for at least fifteen minutes.

Mandy Kettler popped her head in Saundie's door. "You girls better start heading down to the lounge. I hear Westward is a stickler for starting on time." Mandy fit in perfectly on the playground with her fifth grade boys with her haircut and football jersey of the day. Visitors at the school often mistook her for a student because she wasn't much taller than the kids.

"Yeah, yeah." I sat up to put on my shoes. "Let the witch wait, I've got to make a pit stop."

Splashing water on my face, I knew I was as misplaced in an elementary school as Paris Hilton in a thrift store. I refuse, absolutely refuse, to dress like a stereotypical teacher. That means no apples, no teddy bears, no awful sweater vests. I'm only twenty-four and I like to think I have some fashion sense. This happens to make me stand out among the long-jean skirt, apple wearing teachers that populate the other five classrooms. I have long blonde hair and the audacity to actually apply a little eyeliner in the morning. This makes the other teachers hate me. Like I dress them every morning.

In the middle of reapplying my mascara, Miggy's voice boomed over the intercom. "Dottie Gale, if you are in the building, please head to the teacher's lounge. The entire staff is waiting for you." She emphasized the word *entire* like I was holding up a briefing with the President.

Taking a few extra minutes to add the exclamation point to fashionably late, I wandered down the hall to take my place in the cramped quarters of the modular. I didn't even glance at Westward as I sat, but crossed my legs in my short black skirt and offered a piece of gum to Mike. He shook his head, his eyes glued on Westward, not even taking the time to check out my legs. First Mandy … now Mike. This woman had everyone scared stiff.

"So nice of you to join us, Miss Gale." Westward's smile lingered on her face, sticky sweet. I tilted my head, picturing Westward with a forked tongue and venomous fangs slithering down the folding table. "Please try to be prompt to our next meeting so your teammates know you value their time."

Forcing my best fake smile, I held up my notebook. "I'm ready to go, boss. You'll find that I'm a team player."

"I'm happy to hear that. Since you're taking notes already, I'm sure you won't mind typing up a report tonight and putting a copy in everyone's mailbox first thing in the morning." Westward turned toward the white board. "Since you're a team player and all."

Miggy beamed, tossing her staff meeting notebook onto the table, free from her secretarial duties.

This woman was playing for keeps, and no matter how much I wanted to turn into Saundie and blend into the wall paper, my personality made me the centerpiece of the table—which at the moment happened to be a salt and pepper shaker and a September edition of *Education Today*. Maybe keeping my mouth clamped shut for the rest of the meeting would help.

"Now that we're all here, there are three things I'd like to discuss on today's agenda." Maxine wrote evaluations, classroom management, and differentiated instruction on the board. I slumped down in my seat, ready to take a snooze, but the cold metal under my bottom made it impossible.

"You all know that I'm starting teacher evaluations this week. This will begin the process that will culminate in May, on whether or not to recommend your rehire to the board. Looking over Mr. Rollins' evaluation form, I find it highly inadequate for evaluating the standard of teaching we expect here at Quandary Elementary, and in the state of Kansas."

Mandy raised her hand. In the glow of the cheap fluorescent lights, she seemed to be shaking. Highly unusual.

"Yes, Miss Kettler?" The way Westward raised her eyebrows I wondered if she welcomed questions at all. Mandy, normally a very tough person, looked unnerved.

"I was on the committee that came up with the evaluations the school uses. We collected multiple samples from around the state and then tailored the evaluations to meet the needs of our school." Mandy took a swig from the soda bottle in front of her before continuing—a sign that she was backing down. "They are excellent indicators of teacher performance."

Mandy's words, although strong in content, came out in almost a whisper as Westward stared her down. I recognized the same daggers that I received on numerous occasions.

"But of course, it could always be improved on." Mandy slouched in her chair refusing to look any of us in the eye.

"When I enter your classroom, I need to see your lesson objectives clearly stated on the board." Westward brandished her red marker. "We will meet during your planning time the following day to discuss your effectiveness as a teacher." She checked off the evaluation part of the agenda. At least her efficiency kept the meeting moving.

Sue Fox, the kindergarten teacher who was anything but a fox, in looks or cleverness, raised her hand. Her long cream sweater dress hung like a sack of potatoes, her glasses perched on the end of her nose, her cheeks rosy from the fact that she never spoke at staff meetings.

"I want to discuss the behavior I see in some of the classrooms and in the hallways." Westward sneered.

Sue kept her hand raised and started to wave it around like an impatient kindergartner. It made me wonder if she had to use the potty.

"Yes, Sue. We have exactly twenty-three minutes left for this meeting and I don't really have time for questions." Maybe *patronizing* was a quality the board looked for in the new principal.

"Oh, I understand, Ms. Westward." Sue tugged at her sleeves refusing direct eye contact. The words escaping her mouth surprised Sue as much as it surprised the rest of the room. "It's just that I don't think going over lesson objectives will be effective with five-year-olds." She glanced up, clutching and unclutching her water bottle.

Westward's lips curled up in the corners, flashing a smile faker than an aging Hollywood star's face. I gripped the edges of my metal chair, anticipating the venom attached to that smile, but she just turned back to her agenda. Sue looked down into her lap. Her red cheeks were a sharp contrast to her white knuckles that gripped her water bottle. I imagined Sue as one of those people that would end up on the nightly news, killing five or six people and possibly herself. You can only stretch a rubber band so far before it snaps. I know because a few boys in my class have welts on their hands from trying.

"Some of you either need a course in classroom management, or a pink slip." Westward dropped her red marker in the middle of the table. "I'll leave it at that."

While Westward crossed the second item off her agenda, Corbin Lane strolled in and sat down next to Miggy, causing a slight stir in the room. Board members came to board meetings, not staff meetings where everyone was bored. Of course, this one was slightly more interesting than the first thirty or so I attended in my career. Glancing over in his direction, I offered Corbin a quick smile, which he returned with his own slow, lazy grin. I lowered my eyes and pretended to take notes.

"Perfect timing, Mr. Lane." Westward's fake smile was plastered on her face again.

Even though I knew that Westward resented having a twenty-six year old board member as her boss, she still knew he held one-fifth of the power. She beamed at him like a brown-nosing champion. "I was just about to move on to our last agenda item."

"Do you mind if I present it to the staff?" Corbin's dark hair fell into his face again today, and he wore his black work polo with the emblem from the Dive embroidered on the front. The back of the shirt, hidden against the chair, read *Dive in for a Good Time*. Corbin owns the local hotspot. He opened it a few years after graduating from high school. That, along with his good looks, made him a sought-after bachelor in town. Women old enough to be his mother chased after him.

Westward's jaw hung open. "I suppose it's best since you're funding the trip."

A few staff members, that I'm sure were sleeping at this point, straightened up. A trip usually meant a jaunt over to the local history museum with a bunch of pre-adolescents, and a picnic in the park trying to keep the students on the play equipment and away from the pond. The young ones liked to chase the ducks and accidently fall in, while the fourth and fifth graders liked to chase each other and intentionally fall in.

Corbin moved to the front of the room and shifted his weight from one foot to the other for a good thirty seconds before Westward sat down next to Sue.

"Well, from the look on all of your faces, you probably think I'm going to talk about a field trip, and in a way, it is." After allowing a moment of groans, Corbin continued. "It's kind of a working field trip for adults and one of you gets to go."

"It's a conference on differentiated instruction." Westward just couldn't keep her big trap shut and let somebody else have the spotlight for a few moments.

I rolled my eyes, but Corbin had the patience of a school bus driver. He smiled at her.

"What type of instruction?" Wanda Jo piped up for the first time from the doodles in front of her. Dozens of cartoon characters now existed because the principals made Wanda sit through staff meetings. Her shift at the Dive started right after the meeting, so she wore the same shirt as Corbin.

"It's really teacher talk. Finding the best ways to meet the needs of each individual child." Corbin surprised me with his educational knowledge. Westward kept her mouth closed this time. "This year's conference is being held in Las Vegas."

The room exploded into ten different conversations, each edged with excitement. Heading to Vegas for someone in Quandary, was like seeing the world after never leaving the house. I didn't have the money to go on a trip, let alone pay my bills. My mind began to swirl with possibilities. Growing up in a small town, you can develop a debilitating brain disease called *I hate this place, it sucks.* Most likely other places are worse, but I'd never know, because the furthest I'd been was Oklahoma City.

"The lucky teacher," Corbin paused as the support staff groaned this time. "The lucky teacher will spend four days and three nights at the Emerald City Hotel and Casino where the conference is being held. Ms. Westward and I are also going to the conference. When we come back the three of us will talk about ways to apply the strategies we learned with the rest of the teaching staff."

Mandy leaned forward. "So who gets to go, Corbin?" The rest of us looked at him eager to hear the answer.

Westward stood up again. "I've devised a system based on a series of points you can earn through your evaluations, committees you serve on, and board meetings you attend."

"Actually, I'd rather decide right now." Corbin held up a jar that was used to hold pencils on the counter of the office. "The conference is next week and I want to allow the teacher who is going time to pack and prepare lessons for a substitute."

Averting her eyes from Corbin, Westward plopped back down in her chair. "Apparently, this is your show, Mr. Lane." Continuing to keep her eyes off of him, she waved her hand in a degrading flourish. "Do as you please."

Corbin held up the jar again. "I put each teacher's name in here once." He placed his hand over the opening and shook up the pieces of paper inside before walking to the back of the room. "Miggy? Will you do me the honor?"

Miggy reached into the jar to pull out one of the pieces of paper. She unfolded it and snickered. "You're kidding me. Are you sure this isn't rigged?"

Corbin took the piece of paper, looked at the name, but surprise never swam through his eyes. "You've always known me as an honest man, Mig."

"Are you going to let the rest of us in on the secret?" Westward still slouched in her chair like a pouting child. Placing the turtle shell reading glasses on her nose, she got up, crossed the room, and took the piece of paper.

"My, my, it looks like Miss Gale is going to Vegas." Her evil smile crossed her lips, but her eyes exuded displeasure.

Biting my lip, I was speechless for the first time in my life. My heart screamed as it beat rapidly against my chest. I always dreamed about winning the lottery, my ticket out of this town, but I never knew how amazing it would feel when it actually happened. Picking up my schoolbag, I stood up in a daze not caring in the least that the meeting wasn't adjourned, and walked toward the door. I stopped in front of Corbin. The room was silent as I looked into his endless blue eyes searching for the punch line to wake me up from my dream. When I didn't find it, I lifted my bag to my shoulder, and went out the door.

Chapter 3

Packing for a trip is a lot like perusing the selection at your local bookstore. I pulled my beige pantsuit out of my closet, holding it up in front of the mirror. Gathering my hair in a loose flip, I pinched my lips into a model's pout. This was my informational nonfiction selection, which let the other conference attendees know that I was serious about my profession. Rummaging through the shoes on the floor of my closet, I threw in my brown pumps to finish off the ensemble. I pulled two short summer dresses out of my closet and placed them on top of the pant suit. It's important to have a couple of easy-reads around when you don't feel like being serious. Finally, I walked to my dresser. It took me five minutes to excavate my pink bikini from the mountain of undergarments. I also found two pieces of lingerie, which represented the steamy romances that graced my bookshelf, but seldom played out in real life. To top it all off, I threw in my Converse for good luck.

My luggage sat out on my bed, packed to the rim, and ready to hit the road. The entire plan ran through my mind while I drove home from the meeting. I knew Las Vegas was always looking for teachers, and I knew I was looking for what Las Vegas had to offer. We were perfect for each other. Sitting at my computer, I pulled my resume up on the screen. I read it over for errors and updated my time in Quandary. As I placed five sheets of ivory parchment paper into my printer, the phone rang. Hitting the print button with my cursor, I ran over to answer it.

"Hello?" I glanced over to check on my printing. The track that ran the paper through liked to malfunction causing paper jams.

"Hey, congratulations." Saundie's voice sounded overly happy, maybe to mask her obvious jealousy. "You're lucky Rick's not going to be in Vegas that weekend or I'd have to beat you up and take the plane tickets from your lifeless hand."

"Like that'd ever happen. You know I could whip you, Saundie."

"Let's go out and celebrate. It's ladies night at the Dive."

"Then … you're not mad? You don't think Corbin planned the whole thing?" After Miggy's comment about my name being picked, I wondered if the other teachers really thought it was rigged. Honestly, I wouldn't put it past Corbin, and I had to admit that I knew him better than anyone in Quandary. Maybe others couldn't read him so well.

"Of course not. I'm not saying that I wouldn't love going to Vegas, but maybe I need to save up my money, or find me a sugar daddy like you."

"Shut up. I'll meet you there in an hour."

～～～

The Dive was pretty busy for a Tuesday night and it was hard to find a place to park. I stepped out of the car, grateful that I pulled my blue sweater over my tank top before heading out.

Corbin converted the old general store keeping a lot of the authentic pieces of the building. He received money from the state to help him restore it and paid for the rest through a loan. It was the place to be any night of the week in Quandary.

The music blared from the jukebox in the far corner playing some song I vaguely remembered from when I was in high school. Corbin's best friend Theo served drinks from behind the long bar that ran adjacent to the front door. He raised a dark eyebrow at me when I passed the bar, so I shot him a quick wave.

The Dive had a western theme, and even a small dance floor and stage for Friday and Saturday nights. Most of the people at the bar were locals, but you could always count on seeing one or two strangers passing through. I waved at a few more familiar faces as I made my way to the far end of the bar to order a drink and wait for Saundie.

Theo finished pouring a couple of beers before coming over to see me. "Corbin's stuck in the back tonight. He's got a ton of catch up work to do before he can leave for Vegas."

"I'm not here to see Corbin." I acted appalled that he'd even suggested such a thing. Theo went to pour me an Amber in a chilled glass.

"All I know is things don't flow as well when you walk through the door." He smiled. "It's like his brain doesn't work quite right when you're around. When are you going to get over yourself and forgive him, Dottie?"

"When you stop sticking up for him and putting your nose where it doesn't belong. By the way, when are you going to ask Felicia to marry you? You've only been dating for fifty years."

"Alright, I can take a hint." Theo left to wait on a new customer several stools down.

Percy Jones, the local drunk and vice president of the school board, sat three stools away too far gone to notice me. He didn't campaign under that flag, but in a town as small as Quandary, it's a well-known fact. Percy is as old as hell, and smells like a still. At school board meetings, the first four or five rows remain unoccupied until the standing room only spots are taken. Wanda Jo is Percy's niece. She spends half of her time at the Dive keeping drinks away from her uncle.

"Hey, good looking." A man, probably in his mid-thirties, sat down next to me.

Sometimes I hate going to bars because I feel like a bloody piece of meat in a tank full of sharks. This shark wore his brown hair in a crew cut. A smattering of freckles ran under his eyes. He was very large, like a linebacker, and obviously not alone because he looked back at three men sitting at a booth by the window. All three sets of eyes were on me.

"Hey." I kept my eyes on my beer. I thought about an escape to the bathroom, but I didn't want to miss Saundie. I glanced over at the door, hoping she would hurry up and get here before I had to throw my beer in the shark's face.

"Can I buy you a drink?" I glared at him, raised my eyebrows, and held up my almost-full glass. The painfully obvious was too much for the dim-witted.

"Well, how about joining me and the boys in the booth?" I held myself together. I didn't want to create a scene that my overtly aggressive side desperately wanted to cause.

"I'm meeting someone." I crossed my legs away from the man, a clear psychological turn-off according to *Vogue.* "But thanks for the invite." I lifted the glass to take another sip when I felt a hand on my shoulder. Crap. Why did they always have to cross the line into my personal space?

"Come on, it'll be fun." He refused to give up. I shook off his hand, ready to tell him what I thought about his fun.

"Is everything alright, Dottie?" Corbin put his hand on my arm, but this time I didn't pull away. An idea popped into my head. I reached for his other hand and held it in mine.

"Sure thing, Corb. I just told this gentleman that you were on your way." I put on the fake smile that I usually reserved for Westward. "This is my boyfriend, Corbin. I don't believe I caught your name?"

"Leaving." The man sulked back to the brotherhood. The other three men were suddenly fascinated by their beer glasses.

"Thanks." I let go of Corbin's hand. "He wouldn't give it up."

Corbin stood there for a moment, and I could tell his mind was elsewhere. He reached down and took my hand again before setting his eyes to me. "I actually wanted to talk to you about something. Do you have a minute?"

"I'm supposed to meet Saundie." I looked at the front door. A young couple came in with their arms around each other, trying to warm up from outside.

"She called about twenty minutes ago and wanted me to tell you that she couldn't make it because she had to babysit for her sister."

"Well, thanks a lot." I slapped his arm with my free hand. I hated Corbin for hurting me, but he was still my best friend and that came with slapping rights. "I've only been sitting here waiting."

"It's been busy tonight, Dot." His face was tired, and for the first time dark circles formed under his eyes. He caught me looking at him. "So, *now* do you have a few minutes?"

"As long as you do." I hopped down from the stool, but still held onto his hand.

We weaved through the tables toward the back of the bar. Wanda Jo stood in the busiest section taking an order. Her curly brown hair poked out in two short ponytails near the top of her head. She winked at me when she saw Corbin leading me by the hand.

He called to her across the room. "Wanda, I'll be upstairs if you need me." We made our way to the stairs and the living space above. It was the only space, other than the bathrooms, to get any peace and quiet.

When we reached the top of the stairs, Corbin pulled out his key ring and unlocked the door to his apartment. It opened to his kitchen where a dim light shone above the stove. Even after he closed the door I could hear the blaring music below. The Macarena. I folded and unfolded my arms, swaying my hips to the silly song. Corbin sat down at his kitchen table watching my corny line dance.

"So this is where all the action happens?" I wiggled my hips a second time through before collapsing into the chair next to him.

The kitchen walls were covered with barn wood, but the overall look of the room was very simple. The only decorations were an old fashion clock from Germany and some machinery gears above the table.

Corbin reached his hand across the table and took mine again. His eyes, even in their haggard state, held the same longing.

"So, was that drawing rigged today?" I pretended that I was immensely interested in the wine barrel saltshaker at the center of the table. Sliding it into my free hand, I kept my eyes averted as I waited on an answer.

"What do you think, Hottie?" He started to trace the shape of my fingers, stopping to rotate my ring that always seemed to be facing the wrong direction.

"You know I hate that name." One of my nicknames in high school was Hottie Dottie, which I found highly unoriginal and immensely annoying. I later learned that another nickname I had was Snottie Dottie. It was courtesy of Samantha Kearn, whom I'm happy to say is now working in a woman's prison, where I'm sure she has earned plenty of nicknames of her own.

"I know." He looked up from his finger tracing. "But I can't help it if it's true."

The saltshaker fell, spilling the crystals across the table. Keeping with superstition, I grabbed a pinch and tossed it over my shoulder. I stood up, pretending to be interested in the odds and ends on his refrigerator—a calendar from River Bank and Trust, a picture of his niece and nephew taken at Disney World, the work schedule for the Dive.

I heard his chair move, and then I felt him behind me. His breath warm on my neck. My body reacted with wanting, but my brain kept shouting the opposite.

"I'm sorry. I promise to be good." His voice came out as a whisper.

Turning toward him, I found his face inches from mine. I gulped. I closed my eyes, not in anticipation of a kiss, but to steady myself. "Yes."

Corbin took a step back looking confused. "Yes?"

"I mean yes, I think you rigged the drawing." I walked toward the counter, out of kissing distance. "But

I guess if you're paying for the conference, you can do what you want."

He ignored my comment, moved toward me and opened the cabinet above my head. I froze, feeling his body against mine, causing my brain to continue its struggle with the other less sensible parts of me. He pulled down a glass and walked over to the sink, knowing perfectly well what he was doing.

He filled the glass and lifted it to his lips. My gaze fixated on his neck, his chest. He placed the glass in the sink and then turned to me. "So do you want the grand tour?"

I nodded, unable to speak for once in my life.

The apartment consisted of three rooms: the kitchen, the bathroom, and his bedroom. Since we already covered the kitchen, we moved onto the bathroom. Like what I had seen so far, it was very simple. It held a sink, toilet, and bathtub, which were all the necessary components. The surprising part was that it was all so well kept and clean. Growing up, his mother was constantly nagging him to keep his room tidy. Finally, we reached the bedroom. It goes to say, that the tour didn't last very long.

The bedroom was smaller than mine, but fit a queen-sized bed comfortably centered between a pair of mismatched nightstands. Corbin built two rows of bookshelves beneath the window that overlooked the parking lot. Sitting between Hemmingway and King was a wooden frame containing a picture of me lounging on the porch swing in front of my house. It was taken on Corbin's fourteenth birthday with a disposable camera his mother gave him.

"So what did you want to talk to me about?" I crawled up beside him on the bed, placing my legs over his. It felt comfortable, like hanging out with my old childhood friend, instead of the jerk that cheated on me. The tension from the kitchen was gone for a few moments.

He shifted his body to the side, facing me, entwining his fingers with mine. Corbin's dark hair fell across his forehead, in stark contrast to his pale eyes that happened to be looking at me like I was the only thing that mattered in the world.

But then he said the last thing in the world I expected him to say. "I didn't do it."

"What are you talking about?" I ran my finger along his arm.

He continued his gaze, as he lifted his hand caressing the side of my face. My heart rate increased, and I knew I had to get out of there before I did something dumb. But I waited to hear the answer to my question.

Corbin sighed, rolling onto his back again and stared at the ceiling. "I didn't cheat on you with Wanda Jo."

At this point my temper culminated past its boiling point. I bolted upright. "Don't you even lie to me! I saw you."

I grabbed my sweater and stormed to the bedroom door. "And don't think anything is ever going to happen between us. You're a liar and I hate what you stand for!"

He rubbed his eyes, the weariness from downstairs taking over again. "And what do I stand for?"

I lowered my voice to a whisper because it was the first time I had spoken the words aloud. "Corbin, you have roots dug deep into this town, and the only thing I want in the world is to get out of here. I can't be tied down by you." I knew my words hurt him, so I slammed the door to add to the drama.

Chapter 4

2002

Quandary Pond was situated between my house and the tiny one-bedroom shack that sat five minutes down the road. The shack was a rental, and a poorly cared for one at that. Our neighbors didn't stay there much longer than a barefoot on the pavement outside Price Chopper in July. The house appeared lopsided to me, shingles falling off and the siding was worn with time. Grass grew as high as my thigh, and Uncle Embry often stated his intention to go over there and give the yard the weed whacking it deserved. The last residents had left in the middle of the night. I overheard Aunt Henrietta say something about drug charges.

"I'm going down to the pond!" The screen door shut behind me. Uncle Embry was at work at the air-conditioned post office and Aunt Henrietta reclined in the oversized recliner trying to stay cool in the heat of the Kansas afternoon. The fan that oscillated next to the chair made more of a racket than what it was worth.

I preferred cooling off by the pond. Dressed in cutoffs and a tank from the local thrift store, my braids bounced against my back as I skipped down to my favorite hangout.

Making my way down the path from the house to the pond, I glimpsed a red station wagon sitting in front of the shack. New renters. I never really took the time to get to know anyone who lived there, since they'd probably be gone in a couple of months. Removing my shoes, I dove into the pond, no longer worried about the leeches that some of my girlfriends squealed about.

After a short swim, I trudged out, settling on a drip dry as I made my way to the tree where I hid my stash. The hollow in the tree contained a jar for bug catching—usually fireflies at night, a couple bottles of water, a net, a pail and my science journal—which I kept in a plastic bag in case it rained.

I took out the net and started to creep around the reeds looking for Old Bill, the bull frog that was as large as a grapefruit and had so far avoided capture. My goal was to sketch and categorize each frog in the pond, as well as many of the insects.

Rounding the bend by a large tree, Bill sat on a rock sunning himself. This was going to be the day. A crop duster flew overhead masking any sounds my feet made in the grass. I lifted my net at the perfect angle for frog catching, ready to pounce.

"Are you trying to catch that frog?"

Old Bill jumped off the rock and back into the depths of the pond. I could almost hear him laughing at me from the murky waters.

I whipped around in anger, ready to attack the big mouth with my words. "I was until you had to open your trap and scare him away!"

"I'm sorry." The boy was older than me, and definitely not someone from my school. He had dark hair—almost black like the new tar they laid on the main road through town. A smattering of freckles dotted the bridge of his nose, probably the kind that the sun brought out in the summer. "Do you want me to try to catch him?"

"No," I muttered. "Just go away. This is my pond."

"The map the realtor gave us said it was called Quandary Pond, I must've missed the sign." He paused and grinned. My fist had knocked that type of grin off a couple of boys' faces before. "What's your name anyways?"

"If I tell you, will you go away?" I kept my back to him determined to at least find a tadpole and shake away the annoying fly behind me.

"Maybe," he said, still following. I reached the shore near the trail and set my net against a tree, refusing to reveal my other treasures.

"I'm Dottie." I turned to start up the path to go home. "Are your parents renting the shack?"

"My mom and I just moved in yesterday." He didn't follow me up the path, but drew some letters in the mud on the bank with a stick. "I'm Corbin."

"Nice to meet you." I reached the crest of the hill. "Now stay away from my pond."

"Hey, Dottie!" Corbin ignored my comment. I turned and rolled my eyes. The other girls at school would find him cute.

"What do you want now? Pond's not for sale, so don't even ask." Corbin pointed to the letters he drew in the mud that read *Dottie's Pond*.

"Just in case someone else doesn't know, thought I'd save them the trouble of having to deal with you." Corbin threw his stick into the water and went back to the rental.

The next day I walked down to my pond to look for Old Bill again. It was after dinner and the croaking from the frogs echoed all the way to my house. My plan was to search the reeds for Bill, and then if luck escaped me there, to pull out my bug jar to catch fireflies.

Aunt Henrietta took me into town earlier in the day to visit with my friend Wanda Jo from school. She told me she wanted me to socialize with other girls, so I wouldn't turn into a tomboy who flopped around the pond all summer. I had on my long pants from the visit and a blue cardigan sweater she threw at me as I ran out the door after dinner.

I didn't expect that the new boy would come around again. Many of the boys at school found me pretty, so I continuously worked on ways to discourage them. I refrained from combing my hair for days, didn't brush my teeth on a regular basis, and wore clothes that were too loose on my changing body. Of course, once Aunt Henrietta got a hold of me, everything was straightened back out. Many times I had to resort to using my words to crush their spirits. I smiled to myself thinking about how I kept the new boy from thinking he might have a friend.

A wooden sign was nailed to the tree where my stash lay hidden. In white letters, it read *Dottie's Pond: No Trespassing*. I stopped and surveyed the landscape for human life. Maybe we could be friends.

After two trips around the pond, Old Bill was nowhere to be found, so I traded out my net for a jar. The sky darkened with the setting of the sun, and the first tiny glow of a lightening bug illuminated beside a nearby tree. The darkened outline of the new boy appeared on the path that led to his house.

"Do you think my sign will keep the others out?" Corbin asked, as he drew nearer.

I shook my head. "It didn't keep you out, did it?"

"I just have a feeling that we're going to be friends." Corbin reached into my tree and took out a bottle of water.

My mouth hung open. After gulping down half the bottle, he asked, "How old are you anyway? Eight?"

"I'm nine and three quarters," I sputtered. "How old are you?"

"Twelve. I'll be thirteen next January."

"And you think that gives you the right to march in here and steal my pond and my stuff?" I watched him, waiting to catch him off-guard. With a strong enough shove, I could send him straight into the water.

He turned, looking out over the glassy surface that captured the last pinks of the sunset. Now was my chance. But then he spoke. "No, it's your pond. But maybe I've got the experience to help you catch that frog of yours."

~~~

The events of the night before failed to break my spirit. When I arrived at work that morning I was in a perky mood thinking about Vegas. My favorite band, Toto, blared from the stereo on the counter that ran along one wall of my classroom. I picked up cassette tapes at yard sales and thrift stores because that was the only way I could play music in my Jeep, that also happened to be a dinosaur from the eighties. It had over two hundred thousand miles on it, but my mechanic kept it running as consistently as the little noses in my classroom.

I sang along while I passed out an addition sheet for the students to work on when they got to school. I knew I wouldn't make it on one of those singing competitions on television, but it helped me get through my morning. As I pulled down the last chair from the top of a desk, Westward walked into the room. She stopped the music, yanked out the tape, and headed for the door.

"Hey! I was listening to that!" I wasn't sure what her evil, diabolical plan was this time. Taking someone's Toto cassette was a low blow, even for her.

"I will not allow this trash to be played in the school." When I protested, she cut me short. "I need to speak to you during your planning time today. Don't be late." She left the room carrying my good mood with her.

At ten o'clock, I dropped my students off with Mr. Pellitier, the art teacher. He always had them free draw the first five minutes of class to spark creativity, so he stepped out into the hallway.

"What's wrong, Dottie?" I should have known my agitated mood was written all over my face.

"I've got to go meet with Westward. Does that explain anything?"

He chuckled to himself putting his hands inside his art smock. Stan went to college at some esteemed art school in New York and had dreams of becoming a great artist. But I think somewhere along the line his dream changed from becoming the next great artist to inspiring the next great artist.

"Well, good luck. You know I'm on your side." He walked back into his classroom.

Westward sat at her desk, typing away at the computer when I entered her room. Without a word, I sat down in a big, lilac chair and waited for her attention. The office definitely had changed since Rollins was here. Westward got Mike to paint the walls a pale pink color during the summer break. A signed picture of John Mellencamp hung on one wall alongside a gigantic poster of him in some movie. Animal print linens were used as accent pieces throughout the room including some kind of zebra blanket thrown over the lilac chair I sat in.

She continued to type, so I picked up a picture in a pink furry frame sitting on the bookshelf next to me. Westward's hair was jet black and she had her arm around a woman who looked like her twin.

"Is your sister a principal?"

Westward wore her tortoise shell glasses and her red hair was especially bright today. My Toto cassette sat on her desk like a prisoner held in this bizarre zoo. I even felt bad for Mellencamp.

"No, she's dead and you're late." She continued typing away at her computer.

Instead of handing her excuses, I said, "Yep. What happened to your sister?"

She hesitated in her typing for a moment. The tension that filled the room told me she was ready to leap across the desk, strangle me to death, and add me to her collection. "A house landed on her."

I almost spit out the gum I was chewing. "Did you just say a house landed on her?"

"Yes, I know it must all be highly amusing to you, Miss Gale, but she was my sister and it was a terrible tragedy for our whole family." She didn't look up the entire time, letting me know that my words didn't bother her.

"But … how?" Westward almost seemed human for a moment, like a person with a real family and emotions. I didn't think I could handle this new revelation.

"We live in tornado country, Miss Gale. Use your imagination." She looked at me for the first time. "As you know, the conference starts next Wednesday. If I calculate correctly, you should probably leave this Saturday to give you plenty of time to get there."

"You want me to drive? But that's over a thousand miles!" My little dinosaur made it fine around town, but a drive to Vegas would be the death of her.

"How else did you think you were going to get there?" Now I was the one that wanted to leap over the desk to wipe the smirk off Westward's face.

"Let me see … we happen to live in the twenty-first century. I'm sure a plane might be an effective mode of transportation." I knew she would come up with some way to get back at me for Corbin's rigged drawing.

"If you drive, that will save the school the money for one plane ticket. I also made arrangements through the conference website for you to carpool." Westward picked up a piece of paper off her desk moving her finger down the print. "I have two people I want you to pick up on the way to Vegas. They'll be reimbursing the school for your services. There's a Mr. Fields and a Mr. Lyons."

"And who will be reimbursing me for the gas, hotels, and mileage on my car?" My heart was racing. Westward wanted me to pick up strangers on my way to Vegas. It was one step above hitchhikers. Who knew? Maybe they were homicidal maniacs.

"Your passengers, of course." She opened the window behind her and then picked up a manila envelope and handed it to me. "This envelope contains your hotel reservations in Vegas, addresses to pick up your passengers, and the flight information for myself and Mr. Lane so you can pick us up at the airport Tuesday night."

I grabbed the envelope, slamming the door to her office on the way out. Stan stood outside the art class when I came storming down the hallway.

"Well, I can see that went well." Stan grinned.

"Just give me the kids," I muttered.

The dirt road that led to my house was littered with potholes and washboard from the heavy rains. The town only had money to fix it every two years, so it came to the point during the rainy season that you needed four-wheel drive to make it without a flat tire or punctured muffler. This fact alone prevented me from having many visitors.

That's why it took me by surprise on Friday night when my doorbell rang. I sat at the kitchen table trying to map out a route to pick up the other two teachers on the way to Vegas. To hit the two towns they lived in, I could either take the Interstate or Route 66.

Wanda Jo stood on my doorstep with a brown shopping bag in her hand. Her curly hair sat almost on top of her head in a ponytail making her look more like a teenager than an adult.

"Hey, Wanda. What are you doing here?" I tried to keep any disappointment out of my voice. My long road trip began tomorrow and I already had my bed covers turned down.

"I thought I'd bring a peace offering. You have that hot red dress that I'm sure you're going to wear to the dance on Saturday night." She lifted the bag and pulled out a high-heeled shoe. It was dangerously high and satin red with glistening ruby colored stones. I almost salivated looking at it.

"You don't have to make peace with me." I rotated the shoe in my hand to look at it from every angle. "And who said anything about a dance on Saturday?"

"Well, I checked out the conference website and it mentioned the social in the Grand Ballroom on the last night." She put down the bag and took out the other shoe. "Now stop all this jabbering and try them on."

Placing the shoe on the floor, I took off my sandals, and slipped my feet into the red heels, they glittered in the dim lamplight of the living room. "These are perfect, Wanda. Now I only have to find Prince Charming at the conference to take me to the dance."

"About that." Wanda hesitated, her eyes looking down. "The other night when you were at the bar, I saw the look on Corbin's face after you went running out. He came down the stairs and got back to work, but something in his face changed. So I asked him about it."

"And I suppose he told you that I'm a terrible person." I carried the shoes to my bedroom to pack in the suitcase with my red dress. I lifted the case onto my bed, pinching the latches until it popped open.

Wanda stood in the doorway, leaning against the frame. It was amazing how different we were. She was content staying static and constant, and I was constantly restless.

"No, he told me that you didn't trust him." She moved into the room and sat down on my bed smoothing the covers out with her hand. "That's why I brought the peace offering."

I hopped on top of my suitcase to get it to close again, while Wanda pushed with me trying to squeeze the overflowing contents back into their container. "What do you mean?" I asked when it finally locked.

"He didn't cheat on you." Tears started to form in the corners of Wanda's eyes. "I've been the worst friend ever." She never talked about what happened in high school with me before, but we just kind of let the years melt away the anger.

"When you caught us that day, I forced myself on him. I was telling him about the stuff I was going through at home and he actually listened. It's all my fault." Tears were welling up in her eyes. "I just care about you two so much. I hate that you're not together."

"But why didn't he ever say anything?" I whispered, still unsure if Wanda's words were the truth or a fancy cover-up.

"You know him better than I do, and I know he's not the type to run after you with excuses." Wanda flopped back down on my bed. "He's always there for you, so maybe that's how he shows that he still cares."

The alarm went off way too early on Saturday for a normal human being to be coherent, and any ounce of perkiness was out of the question. Darkness and cold drafts surrounded me as I lay in bed thinking about the day ahead of me. Westward's paperwork said to pick up Shay Fields in Amarillo and then continue on to New Mexico to get my five hundred miles in for the day. Pushing the covers off I thought about the daylight I was burning even before the sun had come up.

Lugging my suitcase out to the car, I felt relief over the fact that I checked the oil the afternoon before, it was still too dark to see much in front of me even though I had my porch light on. Opening the back door, I threw my luggage in and started to head back to the house to lock up. Something caught my attention, like a white surrender flag, on my driver's side door. It was a simple mailing envelope with my name scrawled on the front. I took it inside to read in the warmth of the house.

The envelope bulged in the middle, hinting to its contents, and my curiosity level went up two notches. Ripping open the top of the envelope, I pulled out my Toto cassette elated to have it for the thousand-mile journey that loomed right outside my doorstep.

A note still lay inside the envelope, so I unfolded it already knowing who it was from.

Dottie,

> *When I was in Westward's office yesterday afternoon, she told me that you chose to drive to Vegas. I know this has to do with our conversation the other day. I'm sorry I made you uncomfortable, and I hope this tape helps a little. I swiped it off Westward's desk when she left the room. Maybe you need this road trip to figure some things out, and I hope you find what you're looking for along the way. I'll see you on Tuesday.*

Your friend,
Corbin

I slid the letter into my coat pocket and held the cassette in my hand knowing my need to blast it this morning. I hopped in my Jeep, reversed it into my turnaround spot, and started down my driveway just as the first light entered the sky. A strange and new feeling swept over me passing the outskirts of Quandary, a feeling that my life was about to begin.

Chapter 5

Quandary High held the prom of 2010 at the Hilton in Oklahoma City. For a teenager from a tiny speck on the map, this was the big time. For most of the junior class, it was their first time going to a city. It was a little over a hundred miles away, but it might as well have been a million for our small-town cars. Corbin and I dated, even though he graduated the year before and worked at a car parts store in Ponca City. Working behind the counter at the register, he took in everything, which gave him the business experience he needed to open the Dive.

Corbin put aside ten dollars a week for two months to rent us a room for the night after the prom. Even though I loved him, my mind and stomach lurched at the lies I told Aunt Henrietta about staying in a room with Wanda Jo. My nerves were also on edge over Corbin's expectations. He was nineteen, good-looking, and really didn't need to waste his time with a high-school girlfriend who wouldn't put out. That night after the prom, Corbin fell asleep on the king-sized bed, while I spent half the night over the toilet. The car ride home the next day was excruciatingly silent, and I knew by the time we pulled into Quandary, he was going to break up with me. But the words never came. It wasn't until the next week when I caught him with Wanda Jo that I knew he had moved on.

The city spread out in front of me like a giant cornfield of metal and glass, so out of place in the rolling fields of Oklahoma. My junior prom was the only time I had ever been to the city. Corbin was my world back then, and my world came crashing down with his one betrayal, the betrayal that he and Wanda Jo now claimed never happened.

Glancing at my Jeep's fuel gage, the needle pointed at the halfway mark, so I pulled off to fill up before the gas stations became fewer and far between. The city woke up while I stood at the gas pump, and more and more cars crowded the road. I imagined Vegas with even more life than this Midwestern city. This was the place I had to make my first choice, out of the many I expected to make on this trip.

Should I take the Interstate and arrive at my destination ahead of schedule, or take the road less traveled like Robert Frost? In his life, the road less traveled made all the difference.

When the tank was full, I went into the store to pay for the gas and pick up a few snacks. Going up to the register, I noticed that the man working it was about four feet tall and only his head was visible over the counter. He had dark hair, deep-set eyes, and a red shirt with the name of the station on it. A fresh cigarette poked out of his rolled-up sleeve. But the first and last thing that struck me about him was his smile. It was warm, inviting, and easy to trust. His nametag said Sam.

He pulled himself away from the morning newscast on his television, continuing to smile. "Can I help you, Ma'am?"

I placed my Diet Coke and Ho Hos on the counter, still staring at the clerk. At that moment, I decided to put my first decision up to a coin toss, with Sam as the coin. I hoped he wouldn't mind. My route would lay out before me based on his decision. Maybe the gambling urge was hitting me early.

"Sam, you look like a smart guy. Are you from around these parts?" It helped to know if I was dealing with a professional before I put a small part of my life in his hands.

Two years ago I asked one of my second grade girls if I should wear perfume on a date with a trucker out of Abilene. Sasha recommended that I wear Obsession like her mom wore on dates. Spraying the perfume on my wrists and neck, I thought he wouldn't be able to keep his hands off me. After ten minutes in my Jeep, Mark broke out in a terrible rash with hives and I had to drive him to the emergency room. Sasha was a novice when it came to dating and perfume selection.

"Born and raised in the city. No place like it in the world." Apparently, he knew Oklahoma City, but was clueless to the wonders of the rest of the world.

I was in no mood to argue, so I took the leap. Leaning forward on the counter, emphasizing the importance of his choice, I said, "Look, I'm going to Vegas for a teaching conference. Do you think I should take the Interstate or follow Route 66?"

He placed my snacks in a brown bag, took my money and printed out the receipt. Sam rubbed his hand along his chin where a couple of days' worth of stubble had begun to grow. He was a thinker, which made me more confident in my decision to trust his advice. "Vegas, huh?"

"Yep, the land of opportunity." I flashed him an anticipating smile.

My first impulsive act was in the hands of a total stranger who made his livelihood at the 7-Eleven.

There's a lot more philosophy packed into that idea than one would think.

He lifted up the bag to me. "Been there once. It's alright, but it's nothing like a night out here in the city. Too many people pretending to be someone they're not." He sighed, "But I guess if you have to go, I'd follow Route 66."

"Really?" I put the change into my purse. Even though it was the one I wanted to hear, his answer kind of surprised me. Most people would suggest getting there as quickly as possible to get in a few extra hours at the pool.

"Just follow Route 66." He laid a map out on the counter and traced the road with his finger. "It'll take you where you want to go."

"Ok." I walked to the glass door that led outside. I leaned against the metal bar, before turning again. "Thanks again for the advice."

"I hope you find what you're looking for." Sam gave me a little wave before assisting the next customer.

"But I'm not … " The door closed in front of me, " … looking for anything." The last words I said quietly to myself, so the man grabbing a bag of ice from the outside freezer wouldn't think I was crazy.

Being a two-lane road, Route 66 kept its speed limit at sixty-five, but once I left the city area, I moved along well. The air was warm for October, so I rolled down the window to let my hair blow in the wind.

Elvis and I sang together while I drove over the Texas border. I leaned toward the passenger side and opened the lid to a shoebox that sat on the seat. Rummaging through while keeping my eyes on the road, my hand settled on a piece of paper. My prom picture. Corbin was in his tux, a little too big and his tie slightly on the short side, and me in a royal blue dress that now looked terribly out of style. I tossed the picture out the window as a symbol of leaving my old life behind. The box held items to leave behind—one at each state border. This was a ceremony of freedom between me, myself, and I, and maybe the police officer who had his lights flashing on his motorcycle behind me.

Turning down the music, I leaned over to find my registration in the glove box. I knew I wasn't speeding, at least not enough to attract attention, so this had to do with the picture that lay by the side of the road at the border. Glancing in the side mirror, I saw the officer approaching, so I put on my best ticket-avoiding smile.

One of his hands rested on the door as he drew out his pad of tickets and his gaudy high school football ring glinted in the sun. "License and registration, please."

I handed him the necessary paperwork, but decided to use my feminine powers of persuasion on the former jock.

"Was I speeding, officer?" He turned his eyes on me for the first time, so I ran my fingers through my hair and raised one of my shoulders. He wore one of those funky helmets and brown sunglasses like they did on that old motorcycle cop show from the eighties. But this guy wasn't anywhere near as good looking as Ponch or Jon. The only thing that his expression said was that he wasn't impressed.

He removed his sunglasses. One of his eyes was brown and the other was green adding to his far from attractive image. "Don't play that sexy innocent kitten routine on me. I've seen it all before." He scribbled out a ticket on his notepad. "I don't know what those pansies put up with in Kansas, but here in Texas we hang people for littering."

My heart beat rapidly. Averting my eyes from him, I stared at the steering wheel. A few moments later, he handed me the ticket and strolled back to his car. Still gripping the ticket, I crumpled it into a ball. I was tempted to throw it out the window in front of the officer, but it ended up on the floor instead. I knew I would have to be more careful with my intentional littering in the other three states.

The clock on my dashboard read 2 P.M. when I pulled into Amarillo behind a stinky hog truck. The Texas heat amplified the stench, so I rolled up my window and sprayed an ounce or so of Obsession around the Jeep. It still happened to be in the glove box from the Mark episode.

My paperwork said to meet Shay Fields at the Cadillac Ranch. I knew from a little Internet research that this was some kind of iconic tourist attraction. It wasn't hard to find, so I hopped out of the car to do a little sightseeing while I waited for Shay.

It isn't every day that you see cars sticking out of the field covered in graffiti, so I pulled out my phone to take a picture. To think that I littered with one little picture while this guy was littering with quite a few tons of heavy machinery. I wondered if the state patrol ever thought about hanging him. Sitting down in the shade beside one of the cars, I was grateful for a few moments outside of my car. My moments didn't last long.

A white pick-up truck sped down the road, aiming for every bump along the way. A dot that must have been a person stood in the bed of the truck, holding out his arms like he was riding a surfboard. I thought the teenagers in Quandary were reckless. The truck skidded to a halt right in front of me and the person in the back lost his balance, flying out on the other side.

"Crap!" I leaped up and ran over to check to see if the boy was alright, but stood openmouthed when I realized it was a man holding his side where he landed. My initial reaction was to let him wallow in his own stupidity, but I was a sucker for a person in need.

I bent down beside him. "Are you alright?"

The driver of the truck jumped out to check on his passenger. The huge smile on the older man's face told me that he wasn't too concerned for the surfer.

"That was some ride, Shay-boy! And I thought you'd be a goner this time." The driver looked down at me. "Maybe you're dead because it looks like you got yourself an angel."

Shay wore a cowboy hat on top of his tangled shoulder-length hair. His eyes were still shut trying to keep the world around him out. When he did open them, he squinted, before focusing on me. I kept my mouth set in a firm line, refusing to find any humor in the situation.

"You're right, boss. I think God sent me an angel." He shifted to his side and then sat up, smiling a crooked grin that revealed a perfect set of teeth. Honestly, I was amazed he still had any of them. "You going to show me Heaven in the back of the pick-up truck?"

Without thinking, I slapped him across the face with everything I had in me, but he took it like it was the kind of thing that happened every other day. Standing up, I gave Boss another dirty look before stomping to the Jeep. "Get your stuff, Shay. We need to get to New Mexico."

Chapter 6

Shay opened the passenger door. He hesitated, probably wondering if he wanted to spend the next couple of days cooped up in close quarters with me. When he did sit down, he leaned toward the door. I think he feared I might slap him again.

I pushed a Duran Duran cassette into the player while we drove back to Route 66. For a moment, I was tempted to take the Interstate to get the hellish ride over with, but I knew I didn't want to change my plans just because of the juvenile delinquent sitting next to me.

I finally broke the silence. "Just so you know, I don't do pickup lines."

He continued to stare out the window.

"How old are you anyway? Because I know quite a few eight-year-olds with more maturity in their pinky toe than you have in that whole body of yours." I chanced a peek, knowing that his immature body wasn't that bad to look at.

"Twenty-eight." Shay chewed on his thumbnail, keeping his eyes on the passing scenery. He didn't elaborate. I always pictured twenty-eight-year-olds as married with at least one kid already.

"Who was that guy you were with?" Boss looked to be at least forty, so his behavior shocked me more than Shay's.

"That's Randy. He's the principal at the school I work at." He shot me his crooked grin again and I wondered if I was losing my mind. "I just call him Boss because he hates it."

"What? You mean to tell me that the role models in the Amarillo school district act like a bunch of overgrown teenagers? I can only imagine what Saturday night looks like around here." I shook my head at him trying to suppress a smirk for the first time. Here I was searching for freedom and I was acting like a scolding mother.

"Usually a party with all the teenagers at my house. You know, local bands, crowd surfing, chicken fights in the pool."

"I have a police officer you need to meet near the border. You two would become pals real quick." I turned up the music, unsure if I wanted Shay in my Jeep or dragging behind it on a rope.

"So let me guess." Shay raised his voice over the music. "You're a straight-laced do-gooder who spends her Saturday nights working at the local food shelter and crocheting blankets for the elderly. How'd you end up so boring? Were you raised by a religious cult or something?"

Refusing to shout, I turned down the music again. "It's called responsibility. Maybe you should try it sometime and see what you think."

We rode in silence for seventy-five painful miles to the New Mexico border. Shay closed his eyes and pretended to sleep, but I knew he was faking because the corner of his lips formed a slight smirk when I switched the cassette to the Culture Club.

Before Shay got into the car in Amarillo, I had moved my shoebox to the back seat for our next border crossing into New Mexico. Not wanting another ticket, I pulled to the side of the road after passing the Land of Enchantment sign. Looking around, I wasn't sure what was so enchanting about the desert landscape that surrounded us for miles.I reached back to get my shoebox and then opened the door.

"Are we there?" Shay sat up and gazed outside at the barren wasteland.

"No, I just have to do something."

"Oh, you need to use the little girl's room. I get it." He opened his door, stepped outside and lifted his arms into a stretch. "I could use a break myself."

A billboard advertising the gas prices and homemade cherry pie at some truck stop stood close by, so I hiked toward it with my shoebox in tow. "The girl's room is behind the billboard. No boys allowed." Halfway up the hill, I called back. "Why don't you look at the map and make yourself useful."

Once I was behind the sign, I lifted the lid of the box sifting through the objects inside: the ring from Corbin, my teaching contract, and the letter. Everything that tied me to Quandary. Using a rock as a shovel, I dug a ring-sized hole behind one of the wooden supports holding up the billboard.

One cool summer night by the pond, Corbin gave me the ring as a promise that he'd always be there for me. I stabbed the sharper part of the rock firmly into the ground, rejuvenating the emotions I'd worked hard to cover up the past seven years. Moving the dirt around, I thought about how childish this newfound ritual was, but it helped me to rid myself of any physical reminders. The crimson stone glinted in the afternoon sun as I placed it in the hole and covered it with dirt.

"Did your pet mouse die?" Shay leaned against the sign, his hat pulled low to cover his eyes from the setting sun. "Because I'm licensed to act as a pet burial minister in twelve states, and it would be my pleasure to say a few words."

I had no intentions of discussing my ritual with this highly obnoxious stranger no matter how good looking he was.

"No, and even if he did, it's none of your damn business." I grabbed the shoebox and stormed back toward the Jeep, Shay trailing behind me. The shoebox sailed into the backseat of the car, and then I searched my cassette box for *Toto*, needing something warm and familiar.

"I see you as an orange." Shay stuck his head through the passenger side window. With his hat off, his light hair cascaded around his face, contrasting with the darker stubble on his chin.

"Excuse me? Did you just say that I am a piece of fruit? A round and plump one at that?" This guy sure knew how to start a conversation. I kept my head down, searching frantically for Toto.

"Not the fruit, the color. I paint, so I see the world and people as colors. And I see you as orange." He continued to lean in the window, the tan of his skin radiated in the sun's beams.

"And what exactly does that mean? I don't like to be stereotyped by someone I've only known for three hours. It's kind of like judging a book by its cover, don't you think?" Many gorgeous covers sat on my bookshelf at home, but my favorite remained *Gone with the Wind*. Uncle Embry picked up an older copy at an estate sale somewhere. Without Rhett and Scarlet on the front, it looked brown and boring.

"I'm usually right. Of course it can change, but I like to think I have an artist's eye." He opened the door, settling into the passenger seat. The first leg of the trip he'd neglected to fasten his seatbelt, which must go along with his truck surfing personality.

"Ok, you've baited me. What does it mean?" I stopped searching for my tape and provided him with my full attention.

"Ask me later." He pulled his hat down over his eyes. "I'm tired, and I like keeping women begging for more."

Giving up on Toto, I shoved the Culture Club back into the player, knowing how much it irritated him. I was willing to give him more of my personality, and believe me he didn't have to beg.

Evening fell over the desert, so I searched for a place to stay for the night. Towns were scattered thinner than Wanda Jo's tips on a Monday evening at the Dive. Last year, I showed my class a satellite image of the United States at night. The east coast was lit up like a Christmas tree, showing that the bulk of the population occupied the Atlantic states. I don't remember looking specifically at New Mexico, but I would bet my ruby red heels that the area we drove through was pitch black. When I finally saw lights up ahead, I was bound and determined to find a motel before the darkness of the desert crept up and swallowed us whole.

The Bluebird Motel had a neon sign that was hard to miss. I pulled in front of the office ready to call it a night. "Are you coming?"

Shay seemed more interested in a bar across the road. "I'll be there in a few minutes. Don't rent me a room. I think I'll just crash in the Jeep."

It was obvious that he hadn't spent as long in the Jeep as I had, so I just ignored him and went to the office to rent my room.

The motel room was what I expected—simple and small, but clean. I threw my suitcase onto the extra bed and made my way to the bathroom for a shower. The hot water loosened my muscles. The stresses of the day swirling down the drain into the oblivion of filth. As I was blow drying my hair, I heard a knock on the door. I wrapped myself in my pink satin bathrobe and went to the door, leaving the security chain on. Leaning over, I inched open the door and peeked through the crack.

"Can I come in?" Shay only wore a thin jean jacket and his hands clutched at the arms. "It's a little cold out here and I was wondering if you wanted to go out. It's Saturday night after all."

"I'll unlock the door." The chill of the night air crept through the crack. "But give me a minute to grab some clothes and get to the bathroom."

His eyes lit up. "Are you naked?" He tried to push his head through the narrow space in the door. Instead of squashing his head like a grape as he deserved, I grabbed a pillow from the bed and held it in front of me.

"No, but please give me a minute so I can look a little more decent." Men.

I unlatched the door and ran to the other room with one of my summer dresses. Shay honored my request. I heard him come in as I yanked the dress over my head behind the locked door of the bathroom.

When I came out, Shay let out a low whistle. "I don't believe in love at first sight, but I'll make an exception in your case."

I rolled my eyes and went to the mirror outside the bathroom and started applying my make-up. "So where are we going? I'm sure a big city like this has a lot of hot spots." I took a moment to check out Shay's reflection in the mirror.

He sat on the end of one of the beds with his ankles crossed and his coat off. His long-sleeve collared shirt was buttoned to the top and his jeans appeared to be too large, a change from the tight ones he had on in the Jeep. The Shay I met earlier today flaunted his body like a Victoria's Secret model on Super Bowl Sunday. Maybe oranges weren't his type.

"Just to the bar across the street. I checked it out."

I smiled, thinking that he scouted the place to see if it would be acceptable for me. I couldn't imagine many places where Shay wouldn't be able to fit right in.

~~~

The bar reminded me of the Dive, with its small town atmosphere and blaring jukebox. It was crowded and a live band played from the stage near the back. The music, the alcohol, the men two stepping … wait a minute. "You brought me to a gay bar?"

I was three-steps from the front door, when Shay caught my arm. He tilted his head. "Yes, technically, but they still have alcohol and you don't have to deal with any guys hitting on you. I thought you women liked that kind of thing."

"No, they'll hit on you instead. What's a gay bar doing out in the middle of nowhere?" I didn't even want to hear the answer, I wanted my bed, to wrap myself in the blankets and forget about this day. I couldn't believe I dressed up to go to a gay bar and I definitely didn't want to admit that I dressed up for Shay. His strategic cover-up wasn't to turn me off, but to keep the wolves at bay.

"Just have one drink with me, Dottie." He pointed to two empty stools by the bar. "We can go to bed after that."

"We?" I raised my eyebrows.

A mischievous grin crossed his lips. "Well, that's not what I meant. You're the one with the dirty mind."

He raised his hand to the bartender. The man wore a sequined vest and cowboy hat with leather pants. A pink boa added to his festive look. "Two prairie fires."

"So why am I an orange?" I pushed my hair over my shoulder knowing that unlike the police officer, my female powers worked on Shay.

He reached over and swept a stray strand of my hair over my shoulder. "Because you're full of life. I can already tell." The sides of his mouth crept upward into its crooked grin and his eyes swam with mischief. "And I know if you had your choice, you'd truck surf with me."

"You are so wrong." I picked up the drink sequins man brought over, lifted it to my lips and took a swig. The glass almost fell from my hand as the liquid poison ran down my throat. "Aggh! What is this?"

"Your test." Shay took the drink from my hand and set it on the bar. A stray drop of the prairie fire ran down the side of the glass and onto the napkin below, seeping into the fabric. "To see if you're an orange. I guess I was wrong about you. It's been known to happen, as hard as that is to believe."

"Give me that drink." I mustered three tons of determination into my eyes.

"I don't know if you can handle it. You must be a brown or even a gray." Shay's eyes were laughing at me now. His hat lay on his lap and somehow the first three buttons of his white collared shirt were now open, revealing the definition of his chest below. He was so cocky.

"Give me that drink!" I piled on another ton of determination, knowing he couldn't resist.

The man beside me leaned toward Shay. "I'd give her that drink if I were you. And people wonder why I don't date women. Too emotional."

Shay handed me the drink and I downed it in ten seconds flat, despite the tears that flowed from my eyes. My throat burned and my vision blurred, but I proved that I was an orange, gosh darn-it—which I knew all along.

~~~

When my eyes opened hours later, I quickly closed them again from the pain throbbing through my head. A light coming from the direction of the bathroom radiated through my pupils and directly into my brain every time I lifted my lids. Grumbling, I rolled over and buried my face in my pillow. The bed sank near me, so I peeked at the source of the sinking. An outline of a bare-chested man formed before me as my eyes adjusted. I ran through last night in my head, trying to figure out exactly what I'd done.

"Here." Shay handed me a glass of water and some aspirin.

I put the glass on the side table, and turned on the light. Shay didn't have a shirt on, but he was wearing his jeans. Shielding my eyes from the light and the sight of his naked chest, I held my breath before asking the question that I wasn't sure I wanted to know the answer to. "Did we?"

Shay laughed. "Do you think I'd take advantage of a woman who wouldn't even remember it? You need to be conscious to get the full Fields experience." Looking over at the other rumpled bed, I let out a deep breath.

"Can I show my face in this town?" I shot him an incredulous look.

"They love you, Dottie. After four drinks, you strutted your heels up and down the bar with Mitch's pink boa on." Shay reached into the pocket of his jeans and removed a wad of cash. "These are your tips. I'm sure you don't want to know that they were mostly from women. Of course, I threw a twenty in here after the lap dance."

"Shut up!" I smacked him with my pillow.

"Oh, you're going to play that way." His mouth produced an evil grin before whacking me with a barrage of pillows from his side of the room. After five minutes of childishness, Shay grabbed his shirt and went out the door.

Chapter 7

With our bags loaded in the back of the Jeep, we pulled out of the motel's parking lot a little after nine. Westward's itinerary said we were to spend the night in Flagstaff and pick up Ezekial Lyons the next morning at his house. Shay moved the seat back and picked up my cassette collection, running his finger along the titles. He paused to make a flippant remark a few times, but settled on a Garth Brook's tape.

The sun climbed higher as we passed through towns even smaller than Quandary going through their daily routines. The hometown restaurants were filled with people eating breakfast, children walked to school, dry cleaning was dropped off, and people drove to work to a nearby bigger hole-in-the-wall. Life went on in these little towns, even though bigger and more exciting places like Vegas were out there.

Shay stared out the window and just when I was about to ask him what he was thinking, he said, "Do you think people are happy in hick towns, or do you think they live here for the nostalgia?"

"Well, I'm from a hick town and it may look like a Norman Rockwell painting out there, but it's far from it. Everybody knows your business." The Jeep hit a pothole, bouncing us in our seats. I frowned at the road. It looked like it hadn't been driven on in quite a long time.

Chunks of tar lay scattered and grassy patches grew out of the dirt below.

"I'd love to surf over these bumps." Shay rolled down the window to get a better look. A small fruit stand sheltered under a metal covering appeared on the left-hand side of the road. "Do you mind stopping for breakfast?"

"As long as you don't try to coax me into letting you surf." I gave him my best evil eye that I reserved for my second graders before heading over to the stand.

My stomach growled inspecting the fruit, tempting me to buy one of each kind. I picked up an apple and took a bite. Shay made for the bags of nuts down at the far end. The proprietor sported a Hawaiian shirt and khaki shorts, even though the weather was cool. The large man's Texas Rangers ball cap shielded his eyes from the morning sun, and he wore a huge grin, indicating that his customers were few and far between.

"Hey! You're … " Shay's mouth hung open, unable to finish his sentence. I looked up from the apples to get another look at Mr. Hawaii.

"Yeah, yeah. You going to buy those nuts?" The man's grin vanished as soon as Shay recognized him. His notoriety escaped me, but being in the middle of nowhere, he obviously wanted to elude gushing fans.

"I'll buy them and any apples you can pitch at me." Shay glanced at me for the first time. "Do you know who this guy is, Dot?"

"No, but I'm sure you're going to enlighten me." Sports weren't my thing. Maybe it was because I didn't relish in the drama of overblown addictive soap operas. To spend hours in front of the television, investing my heart into a team that would probably blow it didn't sound like a productive use of my time. Now, if you wanted to hand me the baseball, I'd talk.

"He's only the greatest pitcher of our time. Don't you watch the World Series?" Shay's hero worship was more than a tad annoying because I wasn't the object of his obsession.

I set my bag of apples in front of the baseball god and winked at him. "You'll have to excuse my friend. We don't let him out much and we're still working on his training. Right now he can roll over and fetch, but his human communication is very shaky."

The apple man laughed, but it was still an evil type of laugh that said, "Let me at him."

Shay just ignored my comments. "Just a few pitches? I've got a glove." He started to walk towards the car. "I promise I won't ask for an autograph."

"Alright." The man sighed. "But you have to buy any apple I throw at you." This time he winked at me as he pulled a heaping basket of apples out from under the fruit table. There had to be over a hundred apples in there, causing his biceps to bulge from the weight.

The pitcher picked up his first apple and tossed it toward Shay, who still had his back turned. The fruit made an arch in the sky, landing a foot to his right. Shay jumped, twisting around with his jaw open. With Shay facing him, the man hurled the next apple at him with full force. It was like a bullet out of a gun moving in slow motion. Still gloveless, Shay's years of reckless instincts took over. He rolled himself to the right to avoid the impending catastrophe. Where he stood moments before, the apple made a ball-sized dent in the side of my Jeep.

"Hey! That's my car!" I didn't care who this guy was. He wasn't going to mess with my vehicle.

The man had another apple in his hand, aimed at Shay who was still in front of the car. I really didn't care one way or another if he hit Shay, but I wanted to get out of there to prevent any more damage. I ran to the driver's side.

"Better watch out little miss. I know how to hit a target."

I slammed the door shut as an apple was reduced to applesauce on my window.

Turning on the engine, I rolled down the window and flipped the man the bird, but rolled it back up again as he picked up another apple. This one sailed toward the back of the Jeep. I didn't understand what was taking Shay so long. The apple hit the back of the car with the force of an overgrown piece of hail. Shay appeared an instant later at the passenger side door. He opened it and stepped in with a lumpy mass at the bottom of his shirt.

"Are you crazy? He could've killed you out there!"

"Can't leave good apples behind." Shay grinned, taking a bite of one of the apples he had in his shirt. "We really should call the police, but he holds the all-time strike-out record."

"Maybe you'd be better off if one of those apples hit you on the head."

Beyond the fruit stand, the road took an even greater turn for the worse. I had to drive the Jeep onto the grass on the side of the road to avoid the next pothole. It stretched across the pavement like a giant roadblock.

"Let me drive. I maneuver these types of roads all the time."

I was about to say no, but the alcohol from the night before must have been still effecting my brain. Looking at him, he had an air of responsibility, like he'd take care of me. I should've taken another look at the applesauce stain on my window.

"Alright." I pulled to the side near a herd of longhorns. The land stretched for miles in all directions, making the sky look enormous. It was like we were in one of those giant snow globes minus the snow.

Shay hopped into the driver's seat with a huge grin on his face, like he'd just won the lottery. "I'm glad you've got faith in me, sweetheart." He leaned over and pecked me on the cheek before revving the engine.

"My faith has its limits." I turned to the window to conceal my blush.

The Jeep took off with a jolt, but Shay was an expert at avoiding the crevices that littered the strip of concrete formally known as a road. We traveled at a faster pace than when I drove, which made me more confident that we might reach Flagstaff by nightfall. I closed my eyes, hoping to fall asleep before it was my turn to drive again.

Corbin's face appeared in my mind, but a younger version, maybe fifteen or sixteen years old. He'd just made the freshman football squad, so he wore his blue practice uniform as he beamed at me through the screen door of my house. Every night after practice he came to see me, the scrawny thirteen-year-old, even though I was sure he was making friends at his new school.

Walking through the kitchen doorway with her dinner apron on, Aunt Henrietta scolded him, "Don't just stand there, Corbin Lane. Come on in and have some lemonade."

Uncle Embry and Aunt Henrietta accepted Corbin like a son and he became part of our family. His mother loved him, but she was spread thin working two jobs. She seldom had time to cheer for her son at his games like the other pin-wielding mothers in the county. As Corbin's second family, we missed only one game when Embry broke his arm falling off a ladder.

"Damn it!" Shay's words startled me, and I wasn't quite sure if I had drifted off or if time stood still for the last few moments. The Jeep was stopped, but it tilted at a strange angle.

I opened my door to check for damage. "I thought you said you were an expert driver!" The front tire was blown out on the passenger side, the front of the Jeep rested in a pothole. "Where in the world are we?"

"Who knows? I did see a sign for rattlesnake crossing a couple miles back."

At least he could find the humor in the situation. Cars didn't travel down this stretch of road. That was painfully obvious. Throwing on my coat, I walked to the back of the Jeep to take down the spare.

Shay whistled. "Baby, you are finer than a new set of tires. A woman who can change a tire, now that's sexy."

He sidled up beside me and brushed my hair off my neck. I lifted my leg and stomped on his foot as hard as I could.

"Ouch! What did you do that for?"

"Don't touch me. And I told you that you've got to knock it off with the lame pickup lines." I lifted the wheel off the back of the Jeep. "If you haven't noticed, I'm pretty pissed."

Rolling the wheel to the front of the car, I kept my head down but could feel Shay's eyes on me. When I snuck a peek, he was leaning against the Jeep with a smirk on his face. He looked like he belonged out here, a cowboy to rival the Marlboro man. "Don't just stand there. I need help, and it doesn't involve checking my ears with your tongue."

Shay removed the nuts and bolts from the tire and replaced it with the new one. Uncle Embry taught me how to change a tire when I got my license at sixteen, but this tire was Shay's fault and I wanted him to get dirty. I drove the Jeep into the nearest town to avoid any injuries to my delicate spare.

I pulled into the lot at the closest service station in Santa Rosa and went to talk to the owner about patching my tire. The lining was fully blown, so I had to plop down the cash for a brand new one.

After the mechanic told me he expected it to take an hour, Shay and I walked across the street to Lucky Lou's to get lunch. The welcoming bell jingled above the door when we entered the diner, causing the waitress to look up from her coffee pouring.

"Sit down wherever you'd like," she said while she rushed back to the kitchen. The place was deserted except for an older man at the counter and a girl eating pie by the window. Shay led me to the other window seat.

We watched the mechanic take the Jeep into the service station across the street. Something was written across the back window in white. "Did you write that?"

"Write what?" Shay feigned innocence, flipping through the menu.

"I believe it says, 'Vegas or bust' on the back of my Jeep." I shot my straw wrapper at him. "Well, it looks like we already busted."

"Can you order me a hamburger?" Shay stood up and looked around the diner. "I need to use the bathroom."

I watched him walk away. Even though he busted my tire, I enjoyed his company.

Finding a decent-sounding salad on the menu, I lifted my eyes to discover the girl at the next table watching me. Even though I assumed she was a couple of years younger than me, her make-up added age. She ran her fingers through her dark, pink-streaked curls, seeming to be taken aback that she was caught staring.

"Are you headed to Vegas with your boyfriend?"

"No." I turned pages in my menu. "I mean, he's not my boyfriend."

"Oh." Her smile widened as Shay came back to the table. The girl moved to the seat just behind his, leaning over to talk to him. "Hi, stranger."

Shay turned his body toward her, eating up the attention. "Hey, I'm Shay. You know, your hair coordinates perfectly with my pillow."

I groaned. "That must be the pillow that coordinates with your Care Bear bedspread."

"I'm Tina." The girl giggled. "You're not from Santa Rosa, are you?" Her finger twisted around and around in one of her curls. From this angle, her red shirt revealed her more than adequate cleavage.

"Now, it can't be that obvious." Shay still faced the table, but he tilted his chair to garner as much attention as possible from Tina. I secretly hoped his chair would topple like one of my second graders that I constantly told to keep four on the floor.

Tina pointed to the service station. "Well, I saw your Kansas plates and Vegas written across the back." The young girl turned crimson. "You two just got hitched! She said you weren't her boyfriend but …"

"No, honey." I gave Shay's shoulder a quick love squeeze. "If this was his honeymoon, we'd be hunting grizzly bears in Alaska, not sitting in front of a slot machine in Vegas like a couple of chain-smoking senior citizens."

"We wouldn't be hunting grizzlies." Shay looked at me for the first time in five minutes. "I don't kill animals. Maybe we'd be making love in a tent surrounded by bears under my girly bedspread, but that's a little different. Right sugarplum?" He took one of my hands in both of his and gave it a squeeze.

Tina looked like she might burst into another fit of giggles. "However you define your relationship, you two have more tension built up than me and my step-daddy." She turned back to her table to finish off her pie.

I left my salad half-eaten and went to the restroom to avoid Shay for a few minutes. I wasn't looking forward to the rest of the five-hundred-miles trek.

When I came back out, Shay was alone finishing off his hamburger. The waitress had left the check, Shay's credit card sat on top of it, and my Jeep sat in the parking lot of the service station. My mood lightened slightly.

"I'm sorry, Dottie." Shay tugged at his collar as I started the engine and backed out onto the main road.

"I think that's the first time you've said that to me." I kept my eyes on the rearview mirror. "I was beginning to wonder if your parents brought you up properly."

He responded with a half smile, but there was something behind that smile, something he wasn't telling me. A quarter-mile down the road I saw what that something was, and I raised my hand to smack him again.

"She really wanted to come." He didn't take his eyes off me. Tina waved her arms on the side of the road. Her packed suitcase sat beside her like she was waiting for a bus. I always hated judging people based on first impressions, but like Westward, my gut was yelling at me to hit the accelerator and run her over.

Shay reached his hand across to the steering wheel placing it on mine. "Please, will you do it for me?"

"You mean the man who just cost me a hundred dollars to fix my flat tire? Or the man who got me plastered in a gay bar last night?" My eyes rested on his hand instead of looking at him. He was also the man who said I was an orange, vibrant and full of life. No one had ever said that about me before. I pulled my Jeep to the side of the road.

Shay leaned over and whispered in my ear. "Thank you."

Chapter 8

My mind wandered as the Interstate stretched out in front of me like a never-ending number line. The highway kept ticking away—mile after mile—with Tina's endless jabbering to fill my head. Shay's infatuation with her must have waned because when I glanced over, he had his head on the back of the seat with his eyes closed.

From the parts of the one-way conversation I gleaned, Tina Steele wanted to go to Vegas to be a cocktail waitress. She didn't have the talent to dance or the coordination to be a dealer.

"My goal is to meet a rich man to take care of me. Imagine wearing fur coats, eating out every night, and living in a mansion. Now that's the life. Don't you think, Dottie?"

"Yeah, sure." This must have been the point when Shay tuned out knowing as a teacher he couldn't provide any of the above items. "But don't you think love is important?"

"Not really. I've had men say they love me, but where does it get me? All they want is sex. If I'm going to give them that, I want something out of the deal. A rich man can give me the things I want."

I turned down the radio, semi-interested in Tina's philosophy of love and relationships. Vegas would be a perfect place for her to find what she wanted because she had the looks to attract the millionaire of her dreams. "Do you have a boyfriend?"

"Two of them back in Santa Rosa." Her voice didn't show any shame in this fact. "Well, I guess I just dumped both of them." She turned around in her seat and flipped a double bird to the trucker behind us. "So long, losers!"

Corbin was the closest friend I had back home, and even though I had only been gone a day and a half … I missed him. His dark hair and the way it fell into his face, his blue eyes, and the way he smelled—which was the smell of home—drifted through my mind. When he found out that Westward made me drive to the conference, he would give her some hell. Because that's what he did. He was there for me.

Shay was so different from Corbin, wild and reckless. For me, Shay was the embodiment of everything I was running toward. Quandary was dependable and constant which equaled dullsville as far as I was concerned. Vegas was vibrant and new. Life with Shay did not equal boring. He opened one eye and winked at me, reaching his hand down to turn up the music and drown out Tina. His hand brushed my knee, which was a little too far out of the way to be accidental.

I've always been fascinated with how close the contestants on a reality show became after spending thirty-odd days on a deserted island together. It's almost like the people are part of a family. Maybe they even spend every other Christmas together. Being locked up in a car with Shay over the past day made me understand it better. You have nothing else to do, so you share things with strangers that your chaotic life never allows you to share with the ones you love. That's why no one ever told me that I was an orange before.

"Don't you agree, Dottie?" Tina leaned her head between the seats. My heart still beat irregularly from Shay's touch.

I fumbled for words as I reached my hand to the side, searching for my cassette box. "Um … sure."

"You didn't even hear a word I said, did you?" Tina sat back and kept her mouth shut for a while, which I considered a blessing.

I glanced at Shay. He had tilted back his seat and slumped down in it, his eyes closed.

Nearly a half hour passed before Tina spoke again. I should've known something was up. "Who's Corbin?"

My thoughts turned immediately to the shoebox that I forgot to stow safely away from prying eyes.

"A friend back home." No further elaboration was necessary. I didn't want to talk about Corbin and our complicated relationship with a complete stranger.

Tina leaned forward again, placing her chin on the back of my seat, her mouth inches from my ear. She reeked of some wretched perfume that I usually associated with old women in retirement homes. "Do you think your *friend* back home will be happy with what you found along the way?"

"That's none of your damn business!" I gritted my teeth. "Close the box or you're going to find yourself walking to Vegas." As soon as we crossed the Arizona border, Corbin's letter would meet its match. Literally. *I hope you find what you are looking for along the way.*

~~~

We made good time on the Interstate, and by mid-afternoon we reached the Arizona border. The lot at the rest area was full of cars and trucks resting from their cross-country haul. A brick building with the restrooms and the welcome center attracted most of the crowd, so I walked down the hill to the picnic grove. The shade of a couple of sturdy looking trees looked more inviting.

A family sat at the picnic table under the first tree. The father wore a number one dad hat and socks up to his knees. His three children ran amuck, attempting to hit squirrels with sticks and rocks, climbing trees, and burping soda. He highlighted the map in front of him. I've been known to hang children by their toes for that type of behavior in my classroom. I almost marched down there to give the three children a timeout at the table, but the woman sitting across from the father made me stop. Her head propped up in her elbows, a faded brown head of hair badly needing a new perm, her eyes kept me from interfering. They were brown, bloodshot, glazed over and helpless. Her ego might be blown to smithereens if I stepped in and played super nanny. The far end of the farthest tree was blocked from the view of any casual observer in the parking lot, so I plopped myself down and opened my shoebox.

Corbin's letter lay on top where Tina had left it, folded neatly and in the envelope. Below the letter lay my contract. Looking over at the family, Corbin's promise made me wonder. Perhaps this was me in ten years if I stayed in Quandary, married to a man in knee socks with no awareness of his wife's needs anymore. The flames were short-lived as my contract became ashes on the ground in front of me. Taking out Corbin's letter, I folded it and stuffed it into the inside pocket of my jacket. Then I tossed the shoebox into the trashcan.

Two men looking like they just walked out of a homeless shelter stood by the Jeep with Tina. The heavy backpacks near their feet were made of the same camouflage material as their clothes. One of the men took a long drag on a cigarette and then handed it to Tina, who placed it promptly in her mouth. They laughed over something, and Tina rested her hand on the younger one's shoulder like it was the funniest thing she ever heard in her life. The threesome stood in front of the driver-side door, so I pulled out my keys and went to the passenger side. Shay was nowhere to be found.

"Hey, Dottie! I want you to meet my friends Trevor and Mikael."

I sighed as I rounded the front of the Jeep to meet what she dragged in. I had a feeling this was a regular routine for her. Anyone or anything that gave Tina the time of day was lured into her clutches before she broke their hearts and sent them packing. At least these two guys were already packed.

Trevor held out his hand, which bore a strange resemblance to Matty Reese's, the second grader who constantly had his finger up his nose. My hand remained in my pocket. "Nice to meet both of you. Do you know Tina from Santa Rosa?"

"No." Tina kept her hand on Mikael's arm. "I just met them on the back side of the building up there. They're hitchhiking across the country. Isn't that so cool?"

Shay appeared from the other side of the car balancing three Cokes in his hands. He looked at Tina's new friends warily. Because Trevor and Mikael gave me the creeps, I was never so glad to see him.

"Well, here's Shay. We'd better get going." I took a Coke from Shay's hand and opened the passenger side door.

"Can't they come with us?" Tina picked up Mikael's backpack. How could I tell her that I wouldn't transport these guys two miles given the choice. Which since I had the keys in my hand, it was my choice.

"Sorry guys. We have to pick someone up tomorrow morning and I only have two seats in the back." I tried to make the disappointment in my voice sound convincing.

Shay moved into the driver's seat, which I allowed on the condition that we stayed on the Interstate, and I settled into the passenger side. It felt like we were at a drive-in movie as Tina put her arms around Mikael's neck and pulled him into a kiss. It was far from a Humphrey Bogart and Ingrid Bergman moment.

"Now that is just wrong." Shay turned the key in the ignition. I glanced over at him and cracked a half smile. The two guys left after Tina handed Mikael a piece of paper, probably with her cell phone number on it.

Tina got into the backseat, but it was obvious that she wasn't happy with us. She huffed and puffed a lot for about fifteen minutes before speaking. "Mikael and I had something special," she finally blurted out. "I've never felt that way about anyone before."

I bit my lip and turned my face away to keep Tina from seeing the giggles escaping.

"You just met him!" Shay broke his silence. "For all you know, those two are drug dealers." His responsible tone took me by surprise. He almost sounded like a grown man for a moment.

"Drug dealers are people." Tina put her feet up between our seats. "You know, it's against the law to discriminate." If Tina kept this up she'd take the brainless award away from Shay.

The afternoon wore on in a peaceful kind of way, with Tina asleep in the backseat and Toto back in the tape player. Shay pulled out his conference schedule and we discussed the classes we had in common. He spent a summer on an Alaskan fishing boat, not for the money, but the experience. Two of the crew died that summer, one a seasoned fisherman. Shay stopped talking after that, keeping his eyes on the road and off me.

Around six, we pulled into the Wigwam Motel, which reminded me of something I saw from a children's movie I showed to my students. A dozen or so teepee structures circled the property, attempting to look like an Indian village. Tina's eyes glowed, and she was quickly out of the Jeep ready to rent a room.

I walked toward the office with Tina on my heels. Despite the silent treatment she gave Shay and me in the car, I said, "You know, I don't mind sharing a room with you."

"I need my own room. Don't worry, I've got money." Tina swung her purse over her shoulder and sauntered, swaying her hips back and forth, up to the front door.

I eyed Shay to check on his mood. "Are you going to sleep in the Jeep again, or should I make sure I get two double beds?" Sharing a room with Shay was easier than trying to deal with Tina's boy-craziness. She might make me stay up all night painting nails and gossiping over teen magazines.

Shay snaked his arm around my waist, pulling me toward the office. "If I say that I'll stay in the Jeep, will you get a king size bed?" My cheeks flushed, but I managed to work my way out of his arm.

The office manager wore a full Native American headdress, welcoming me with a "How".

"How do you do. I'd like a room with two double beds please." I turned to flash Shay a satisfying smile, but he hadn't followed me in.

After my shower, the knock that I expected sounded at my door. I gathered my hair into a ponytail, pulled up my jeans, and went to answer it.

"Dinner?" Shay held up a bag from a fast food restaurant. I opened the door wider to let him in, but he shook his head. "No, I'm taking you out to a fancy place."

"But, I'm not dressed for fancy and what about that?" I pointed to the bag. The stain on the side of the bag told me that the contents were greasy and mouthwatering.

"Just hop in the Jeep and leave the rest to me."

Even though my body protested the thought of driving any further, my curiosity won out. Shay's spontaneity attracted me almost as much as his rugged good looks, which at the moment left me in a state of intoxicated bliss. I didn't care if we left Tina behind and drove to Vegas on our own. I just wanted to be unpredictable for once in my life.

We took the exit off the highway into the Painted Desert and drove to a lookout that was empty of other visitors. Stepping out of the car, I caught my breath at the wonderland of reds and oranges brushed by the setting sun. The temperature had dropped from earlier in the day, but I barely noticed because the view was so magnificent. My stomach growled, reminding me of the food in the greasy bag.

Shay brought the bag and a hotel blanket over to a bench a few feet away from a drop off. Resting with one side of the blanket over his shoulder, he opened up the other end for me. I sat down and rolled the blanket around me. My breath was visible in the air. Shay unrolled the top of the bag and handed me a hamburger and fries, which I devoured in six minutes flat. The soda we shared sat on the ground below the bench. When we finished eating, Shay pulled me closer, sharing his warmth.

"Thanks." I kept my eyes on the light show cast by the sun. The brilliant reds and oranges now mysteriously faded into pinks and purples.

Shay rubbed my shoulder with his hand. "No problem. I thought you might need to get away from Tina."

"She'd take every guy in a fifty-mile radius with us if she could."

"That's what makes you stand out from other girls."

I tensed for a moment, not ready for him to turn into Corbin. If he started gushing about how great I was, he might find himself accidently falling off the cliff.

"You know what you want and you go get it. I've only known you for two days, but I can tell a keeper when I see one. You're not the one-night stand I'm used to."

For some reason his words frightened me, and although the phrases were stable and predictable, the words were extremely unpredictable coming from Shay's mouth. Looking up into his brown eyes, I wrapped my hand around his neck to draw his lips down to mine. My kiss intensified, hoping the passion might really get my point across. I didn't want to lose this wild, artistic guy who cared more about his next thrill than seeing the dentist twice a year.

I pulled away, sucking in a gasp of air, but keeping my forehead against his. "But I am a one-night stand kind of girl." Not that I actually ever had a one-night stand, but that was the whole point of this Vegas trip. Every inch of me wanted to fight the hometown girl persona that suffocated me. The girl who married her high school sweetheart, lived in a house with a white picket fence, and had six children playing in the yard with names like Junior and Sammie Mae. Shay wanted what I wanted, to travel the world, never tied down by a marriage certificate. At least that's what I thought he wanted.

Shay pulled away from me to look at my face and then laughed. "You could never be that kind of girl. You're what we call high-class in Amarillo. Most guys would be lucky to end up with someone like you."

"To end up with me. Sounds like the bottom of the barrel." I pretended to be upset, but turned to unbutton my shirt revealing the top of my lacey bra. I dug deep to harness my inner actress, which was no Oscar winner, and turned back to him.

He raised an eyebrow and I hoped his inner caveman instincts were taking over his sexual organs. I took his hand, placing it on my chest.

"Do you want to end up with someone like me, tonight?"

Shay moved his hand, but used it to button my shirt back up. "Leave the pick-up lines to me."

I couldn't handle being Marilyn Monroe anymore, definitely not when he made me feel like Marilyn Manson. I put on my best pout.

Shay held up his hand after finishing the last button and caressed my cheek. "Let's get to know each other first."

I bolted upright "You're the one who wanted a king-sized bed. So please stop pretending that you're so righteous. You act like you're the keeper of my purity or something." I stomped toward the Jeep, throwing the trash in a can along the way.

Shay just sat there. I wondered if he was laughing at me. "I know what I want, and I'm going to get it with or without you. We'll be in Vegas soon, and there'll be plenty of hot guys to choose from."

Shay didn't say anything on the way back to the hotel. He walked me back to my room, kissed me on the forehead, and went to spend his night in the Jeep.

Chapter 9

A loud *riiiiing* woke me the next morning. I wondered if I put in a wake-up call the night before. I reached for the nightstand, slapping at the hotel phone a few times before successfully grabbing it. Holding the receiver to my ear, I was met with a dial tone, but the ringing continued. Must be the cell phone. First light shone in a dusty ray across the room as I leaped out of bed to dig it out of my purse on the table.

Noticeably out of breath, I plopped on the bed. "Hello?"

"Hey, Hottie!" Corbin's voice took me by surprise. I didn't think he even had my cell phone number. In a small town, everyone always ran into their friends; we saw each other around. No need for cell phone numbers.

He was in an irritatingly good mood. "How's the road trip going?"

"Oh, you know, the usual. Road kill, potty breaks, and hitchhikers. Pretty uneventful." I wondered if he knew about Westward's quest to break me. His note told me he was unaware as to why I was driving a thousand miles in a car that could puff out its last toxic fumes at any moment.

"I know I'm not supposed to, but I miss you. You kind of hold things together here." He paused, letting his words sink in. "Westward fired Sue Fox on Friday."

"What?" I turned toward the bed and flopped face first into the blankets. Yes, she was a mouse of a woman, but she had three young children at home and husband who liked to drink too much. "Just wait until I get my hands on her."

"A few of us on the board felt it was unjustified. We're holding an emergency board meeting tonight to discuss Westward's action."

I stared up at the ceiling, the shadows dancing with each wave of the curtain as it met the air from the heater. I imagined Corbin on the other end sitting at the same kitchen table we sat at just three nights before. With work hours away, he'd be wearing a t-shirt and jeans, probably blue, his favorite color. We both sat there in a frozen moment, listening to each other's breathing, neither of us wanting to hang up.

The knock on my door drew me back into reality. "I've got to go, Corb. Someone's at the door. I'll see you on Tuesday."

"Bye, Dottie." His two words were packed with the regret of years of unspoken longings between the two of us, but a second knock on the door kept those desires silent. Throwing a blanket around me, I crossed the room to answer the door.

Shay stood on my doorstep, looking like, well … like he spent the night in a Jeep. His hair stuck out in interesting directions, his shirt was wrinkled, and his eyes were bloodshot. He appeared almost frantic. "We've got problems."

He pushed past me, closed the door, and went immediately to the window where he peeked through the curtains to the parking lot.

"What's going on?" I clung tighter to the blanket around me, wishing I was already dressed. The draft from the door chilled the room, and Shay's unsettled behavior was really starting to freak me out.

He kept the curtain pushed back with one finger, peering into the sliver of daylight. "Just get ready to go."

I unzipped my suitcase and took out a sweatshirt and jeans, then raced to the shower. I had never seen Shay rattled before. His calm and cool attitude helped me get through a flat tire, enabled me to accept a hitchhiker, and kept me from calling the police on the apple assassin. An image of the horrible creature out in the parking lot crept through my brain as the hot water ran through my hair and down my back.

When I came out of the bathroom ten minutes later, Shay was still looking through the crack in the curtains. His hair was tamed, so I knew he used my mirror while I was gone. He faced me, but then looked back outside while he spoke. "I went to check on Tina this morning, since she left in a bad mood yesterday. Those two guys from the rest area were with her. Guess they spent the night."

I shrugged. "So, she's a tramp. We already knew that. It's not like we have to send her Christmas cards after we drop her on a corner in Vegas." Releasing my hair from the towel on my head, I stepped to the mirror and picked up my comb.

Shay stood up, coming behind me, and put his hands on my hips. But in the way he did it, the implication was not sexual, just a way to ground me in the seriousness of the issue at hand. My comb froze halfway through my hair as he looked at me in the mirror.

"They had illegal drugs. Poppies. Opium poppies. Trevor was too far gone when I came to the door, but Mikael knows that I saw them."

"Then let's get out of here. We're going to be late picking up Ezekiel, so the sooner we get out of here the better."

"I picked up the morning paper in the office. They're escaped criminals wanted for murder in Texas. The law is after them, and I doubt they'll let us out of here so easy."

"Well, we could try to leave. If they stop us, then we'll have to turn to plan B." I returned to the bathroom to gather my toiletries and throw them in my suitcase. My heart raced, but I worked on keeping the calm this time.

"And what is plan B?" Shay placed his hand on my arm to keep me from flying around the room in my bizarre state of calm panic. I knew he'd ask, but I wasn't quite sure what to tell him yet.

A commotion flared up outside. Shay let go of my arm and returned to his post at the window again. "The sheriff's here."

I placed my luggage by the door, ready for our escape and went to look out the window from the other side of the curtain. Four armed men with helmets marched up to Tina's wigwam. The grounds were deserted, but the scene commanded an audience. Almost every other wigwam had window peepers trying to catch a glimpse of the showdown. The manager stood in the doorframe of the office with an orange bowling shirt unbuttoned over a white t-shirt. He held onto his morning coffee, a slight grin on his face. Alerting the sheriff to the criminals in the hotel was sure to garnish some kind of reward.

One of the deputies banged on the door while the others pulled to the side, ready for action. "We know you're in there, so open up and it'll be easier on everyone." His voice echoed through the expanse of the motel grounds.

Nothing happened.

The deputy banged again. In what must have been a matter of seconds, but seemed much longer, the officers broke down the door. Mikael and Trevor were brought out first and slammed face down on the ground, handcuffs quickly encircling their wrists. Where was Tina? Did they kill her in the raid or did the murderers do it before the sheriff arrived? My heart went out to the young girl I barely knew. Then she appeared at the door in the arms of one of the deputies and fear no longer held me behind the curtain.

Shay followed, but he didn't try to stop me. I slowed to a walk as I approached the scene.

"You need to stay back!" A deputy with his helmet hiding his face marched toward us holding up his palm. I planted myself about five yards from Mikael and Trevor, but didn't head back to the motel room.

"Ma'am, I'm going to have to ask you to return to your room. We have a situation here." The deputy pushed closer, raising his visor to reveal himself as a man in his mid-forties with a black beard.

"I'm going to do no such thing." I pointed toward the deputy carrying Tina. "That's my friend and I want to know if she's alright."

The deputy's eyes narrowed. "You know these people, ma'am?"

Shay's hand closed around mine. I was pretty certain I could talk my way out of anything as long as it didn't involve the Texas police.

"Yes. I mean no." I gave Shay a nervous look. "What I mean to say is that the girl is traveling with us. I've never met those two creeps in my life." Mikael turned his head in our direction and my stomach dropped. A wicked grin spread across his face.

"Could you stay right here, please?" Deputy Blackbeard went to talk to an older, fatter uniformed man who was sitting in the squad car. The man nodded, and pointed to the two men face planted on the ground.

"This isn't going to be good," Shay whispered into my ear. He put his arms around me from behind as we waited for Deputy Blackbeard to perform a mini-interrogation on the two poppy heads. After a few minutes passed, Mikael pointed a finger in our direction. Crap. It wouldn't do any good to run, so we stood there ready to defend ourselves.

Deputy Blackbeard brought the sheriff back with him this time, pulling handcuffs from their belts as they walked. The sheriff delivered the blow, "You have the right to remain silent … " As the sheriff finished reading us our rights, he pulled Shay's arms behind his back, cuffing him. Deputy Blackbeard just took my arm.

Shay's shoulders slumped. "Can I ask what we did, Officer?"

"We're taking you down to the station for question-ing. Drug possession and aiding and abetting known criminals are serious crimes." The sheriff pushed Shay to the ground next to the real criminals.

"You don't have to be so rough with him! He had nothing to do with this." I glared at Mikael, knowing he was trying to drag us down with him because I refused to let him or his filthy friend into my Jeep.

The sheriff made a grunting noise that might have been deciphered as a chuckle. He spoke for the first time since reading the Miranda rights. "Everybody's innocent. I've had murderers with blood on their hands telling me they did nothing wrong. We've got to have proof to hold you, so we'll see how it goes down at the station."

Two cruisers sat in the parking lot, ready to take the five of us in. They levered Shay to his feet and escorted him to the second cruiser. Thankfully, Deputy Blackbeard led me to the same cruiser because if he put me in the same car as Mikael or Trevor, he might just have to arrest me for murder.

Ducking into the car, I noticed that Shay still had his cuffs on and sat in the middle of the cruiser. Tina was leaning against the far door, but I knew she was alive because of her loud snoring. Now was the time to talk, before an officer took the front seat.

"Call Ezekiel." I said. "He needs to know we'll be late. I'm going to call someone back in Quandary to get us out of here."

Shay glared at me. "Going to call your boyfriend? I'm sure Corbin will come to your rescue. He's got to be better than the brainless loser you found along the way." His words hurt, but it made me understand better why he rejected me last night.

"I never called you a brainless loser. You're not." I contemplated stopping there, but of course my mouth rambled on. "Corbin's a friend back home that I've known for a long time. He owns the local bar, which makes him stable, responsible, and tied down."

"Sounds like every girl's dream." Shay rolled his eyes. "You two make a perfect pair."

"Maybe I want something different." I reached out my hand, touching his knee. "That's what I was trying to tell you last night."

Deputy Blackbeard rounded the car to the driver's side ready to take us all in. Now I just had to decide if I would use my one phone call on Corbin or Westward.

Chapter 10

The Navajo County Sheriff's Office stood about a mile from the Wigwam, near the center of town. In my twenty-four years of life I never got in trouble, and now in the span of two days I had received an outrageous ticket and had been arrested. Glancing at Shay as we pulled into the parking lot, I wondered if the wilder life was a little too much trouble. Deputy Blackbeard and another officer brought us into the building, leading us to the holding cells in the back. Tina and I in one, and Shay, Trevor, and Mikael in the other.

"Sorry to do this to you, ladies." Blackbeard closed the cell door behind us. "Just need to get some paperwork together for the questioning."

Tina paced around the box of a room, refraining from providing me with eye contact. I rested my head against the bars trying to hear what was happening on the other side of the cinderblocks. I worked out ways to get Shay and I out of here, but Tina was the last person I wanted to talk to. She could rot in this box as much as I cared.

A tall, red headed deputy strolled past our cell, and I heard the keys opening the one next to us. On the way back, the officer had a handcuffed Shay by the arm. Shay winked at me as he passed. I sighed relieved to know that Mikael and Trevor left him alone. The door to the cell hallway shut with a loud echo, making me wonder how long the department would question him.

Tina stopped pacing and rested her head on the bars a few feet from mine. I knew she was working out what to say, but I still cringed when I finally heard her voice.

"I'm sorry, Okay?"

A framed puzzle of an English hunting party adorned the wall across from our cell. I kept my eyes focused there, trying to quell the anger that was about to burst out of me and all over Tina.

She moved around the room again and sat on the mattress in the corner. Mumbling came from the other cell. Trevor and Mikael discussing their strategy. My head hurt from leaning it against the bars, but as long as the guard at the end of the hallway didn't meander in this direction, it was my own private space.

Thirty minutes must have passed and Shay wasn't back yet from his interrogation. My legs grew stiff from standing in the same position, so I chanced the short trip down to the other end of the bars. If I didn't look at Tina, maybe I could avoid her lame attempts at an apology. The accidental glance in her direction made me pause. She was balled up against the wall with her arms around her knees. Tears that streamed down her cheeks caused her thick mascara to form streams of black on her skin. A pair of photographs lay on the bed beside her.

I had a momentary argument with myself, before turning toward her out of pity. She wasn't the type of person who let tears flow easily. "Who's in the pictures?"

Instead of the astonishment I expected, Tina's eyes held onto a blank stare, like she was trying to block out everything that surrounded her. She picked up the picture closest to her, gazing at the person captured within. "This is my daughter, Grace. She's six years old and just lost her first tooth." The picture held a girl that was a near reflection of Tina. The girl's dark curly hair was piled on top her head in a ponytail, her face a pale shade of mocha. She wore a bright yellow soccer shirt and grasped a ball in her hands.

Tina put Grace back on the bed and picked up the other photograph. "And this here is my son, Canton. He's two and looks just like his daddy." She continued to hold Canton's picture in her hand while her tear stream turned into a river. "His daddy's in the state pen."

Watching Tina like this, I had no idea what to say. I didn't think she cared about anyone but herself, and she was the last person I could ever imagine as a mother. I took a seat at the end of the bed, next to the girl who couldn't be a day over twenty-two. For someone who couldn't take care of herself, the weight of having two young children must be enormous.

"Where are they?" I asked, trying to draw her out of her sudden catatonic state.

"Back in Santa Rosa. Gracie lives with her dad, and Canton's grandparents won custody of him last year. The court said I was an unfit mother." Her feet dangled off the bed, out of their balled position.

"So why are you running away? Why don't you stay and fight? Show them that you can clean up your life." My vision of Tina twisted and turned as I tried to make sense of her situation. If she was unfit, then why was I encouraging her to take care of these innocent young babies? She flirted with any guy who paid her any attention, and that fact alone could endanger her children. But as we sat here on this board behind bars in the middle of Arizona, my heart went out to her.

"It's not going to happen." She shoved the pictures back into the pockets of her sweatshirt. "At least if I get a job in Vegas, I could send them a nice birthday present. But who knows, I'll probably be behind bars for the rest of my life after partying with those two losers."

The door at the end of the hall opened and I rushed over to the bars to see how things went for Shay. The tall deputy came in without him, but stopped to talk to the guard by the door.

"I'm jealous, you know." Tina walked over to stand next to me by the bars.

"Jealous? Of me?" Right now, I felt like my head was in a mess of indecision. Not a place many would be jealous of.

"Yeah, you've got two great guys. You seem to attract them like I pull in the losers. That's the difference between us. You demand respect and you get it." She smiled to herself. "Maybe sometime you could give me lessons."

"Anytime." I was happy that most of the anger I felt toward Tina had melted away.

The tall redhead finally came to our cell. "Dorothy Gale?"

"That's me. Do I get to make a phone call?"

"Let's just see how the questioning turns out." The redhead led me to the hallway door. I was ready to get through the questions and move on with life. He brought me to a room near the front of the building. Our feet echoing through the hall made me picture myself as a death row inmate. Sweat beaded on my brow. I held my breath, not sure what to expect from the Navajo County Sheriff's Department.

Shay sat in a metal chair at the end of a long table that took up most of the room. Even though other people occupied the space, he was the only one I saw with my sudden tunneled vision. His hands were folded and free.

A smile crept across his face when he saw me. I let out the breath I'd been holding, no longer imagining myself as a dead woman walking.

"Ms. Gale." The Sheriff held out a chair for me adjacent to Shay. "I'm Sheriff Nox. We've just got a couple of questions for you about your involvement with Mr. Smith and Mr. Rennings."

Shifting nervously in my chair, I noticed that the sheriff placed me with my back to Shay. I clicked the heels of my shoes together trying to settle myself. "What do you want to know?"

"How long have you known Mr. Smith and Mr. Rennings, Ms. Gale?" A woman in uniform took notes on a large yellow legal pad. The truth. Aunt Henrietta always said that the truth will set you free.

"My friend, Tina, met them at the border rest area yesterday." I twisted a strand of my hair around my finger in a nervous habit. "She said they were hitchhiking across the country."

The sheriff settled into the chair next to me. My nerves must have been glaringly obvious. "And did you take them with you in the car?"

"Do I look like the type of person who would take two filthy poppy heads into my car?" Sheriff Nox's proximity made me a little too relaxed. I bit my lip, hoping I didn't screw the whole thing up.

"Did you know they had drugs, Ms. Gale?" He leaned so close I could smell the Lifesaver in his mouth. Personal space invasion gave me the creeps, so I scooted back a little ways in my chair.

"No, not until this morning when you arrested us. Of course, Shay and I made all kinds of assumptions about them at the rest area, but that's why I wouldn't let them ride with us. First impressions can be a killer. Like when I first met Shay … "

"Let's stay on the subject at hand." Sheriff Nox pulled back and then stood up, pacing the front of the room. "We've decided to let you and Mr. Fields go. The length of Ms. Steele's detention is still unknown."

After my conversation with Tina in the cell, I knew I couldn't leave her behind. "Sir, she didn't know anything either. She's so young. Her only crime is she is obsessively boy-crazy and attracts the wrong types."

The sheriff put his hands on the table and leaned in. "That may be so, but she knew the two men had drugs."

"But she didn't have a chance to tell anyone. She was passed out from the poppies, and who knows how long she was in that state?" I looked behind me at Shay. He didn't throw me any hint as to whether or not I should proceed, but just stared at the woman's hand taking the notes. "You can't hold her based on what she might or might not have done. You've got the real criminals. Please just let her go."

"So, you believe she was the victim?" Sheriff Nox raised his eyebrows.

"May I say something, Sheriff?" The deputies turned toward Shay, the new voice in the shuffle.

"Go ahead, Mr. Fields." The sheriff nodded. Shay's personality had worked the room before I even entered.

"Dottie was ready to kill Tina and leave her in a ditch to rot when she found out that the two men in question followed us to Holbrook." Shay's eyes met mine. "She must truly believe that Tina is innocent to protect her like this."

"Is this true, Ms. Gale?"

I sighed. "Tina doesn't deserve this, Sheriff. I can hold a grudge as well as the next person, but I won't hold one that keeps an innocent person behind bars."

"I think I've heard enough." The sheriff made his way to the door. Stepping out into the hallway, he closed the door behind him without another word. Did that mean Tina was free?

Deputy Blackbeard stuck his head in the door. "You two are free to go. Ms. Steele will be brought up front to meet you."

Relief rushed over me as I got up and threw myself into Shay's arms. The remainder of the staff cleared out, and we were left alone. Well, except for the one-way mirror. But at that moment I didn't care. I lifted my head off his chest and gazed into his eyes. He pressed his lips to mine, and the horrific events of the morning melted away with the heat of his kiss. Shay could have had me on the table, and I wouldn't have cared, but a knock on the door brought us back to reality.

Shay held my hand as we waited for Tina on the wooden bench in the front office. "You surprised me back there." He threw me a lopsided smile.

"Was it the tongue, or the hand in your back pocket?" I squeezed his hand.

"Well, those were nice surprises, but I meant what you said about Tina. I expected you to throw her so far under the bus that she'd have multiple tire tracks across her body."

"You know I can change my mind about people." I ran my free hand along his arm. This much physical contact with Shay was different, and like a new pair of shoes, I was trying it on for size.

"Did you change your mind about me? Because when you picked me up in Amarillo, I had a strange feeling that you thought I was hot."

"Oh, yeah. A guy lying on the ground in pain as a result of his idiotic actions is always a turn on for me. You must've been hallucinating from the bump you took on your head."

Tina appeared on the other side of the front desk, but her smile failed to greet us. With her backpack slung over her right shoulder, she pushed open the front door and went straight to the Jeep. Blackbeard held the door open for Shay and me, apologizing for the delay in our trip. It was now two in the afternoon and I knew that Ezekiel would wonder where we were. Shay took the wheel so I could make the call to our final passenger.

Chapter 11

Flagstaff was a towering oasis to the low desert land that surrounded it. Tall pines grew out of any spot not covered by buildings or concrete. With Shay's expert speeding we arrived at Ezekiel's place around three. His house was situated in a typical suburban neighborhood, the type where the buildings are so close together you can see if your neighbor needs a shave. The lawn was neatly trimmed, leading up to a hedge of some type of hearty plant that thrived in the dry climate. A white porch swing moved in the wind as if a wayward spirit chose to give up the night for the pleasantries of the day. Thick iron bars ran vertically down in front of each window giving the feel of inner city Chicago, not suburban Flagstaff. An orange tabby cat sat on the top stair daring us to step into his territory, but then moving aside as if he didn't care when we approached the porch.

The front door appeared too solid to be made out of wood, so instead of risking my knuckles, I rang the doorbell. A tiny window within the door opened about two inches above my head, and a set of eyes peered through.

"Who is it?" barked a voice.

"Um … Dottie Gale. I'm here to pick up Ezekiel. Is this the right house?"

"Can I see your identification?"

"Identification?"

"You know," the voice said. "Your license."

"Oh." Of course. I dug around in my purse. Pulling my license out of my wallet, I flashed it in front of the eyes in the door, hoping he wouldn't make a comment about the hairstyle.

The sound of multiple latches being unlocked came from behind the fortress door. I shot Tina and Shay a nervous look. The man that finally opened the door must have been six and a half feet tall, the type of man you wouldn't want to meet in a dark alley. He had a bald head, dark brown skin, and thickly rimmed glasses perched awkwardly on the bridge of his nose. His fully buttoned plaid shirt was tucked into his tan Dockers, giving him the impression of being a complete nerd—even though his biceps told me he could take on the heavyweight champ. He looked to be in his late twenties or early thirties, but his attire reminded me of something Uncle Embry would wear. Underneath the out-of-place clothing, he was an extremely attractive man.

"Hi, Dottie." He must have come from doing the dishes because he had a yellow rubber dish glove on his hand, when he reached out to shake mine. "I'm Zeke."

"Hey, Zeke." We shook hands and I turned to my passengers. "This is Shay Fields and Tina Steele."

He shook both of their hands with his gloved one and then invited us in. As soon as Tina closed the door, Zeke punched a few buttons on his security system controller on the wall.

"I don't usually do this type of thing." He led us to his living room. "My therapist thought it might be a good way to meet other people. After all, who can't handle a four-hour car ride to Vegas by themselves?"

Shay leaned close to me. "And you thought I picked up weird people." Looking around the room, he smiled, "You have a nice house here, Zeke, are you married?"

"Um … no." He adjusted a few knickknacks around the room. Definitely obsessive compulsive. "I'm not very good around women."

"Can't really relate with you on that one." Shay sat way back into the couch and made himself at home. "Maybe I can give you a few pointers. We're going to Vegas, after all. I'm sure you can meet a couple of women there."

Disgusted with the male bonding, I suddenly decided I needed my suitcase. The second I turned the doorknob, all types of sirens filled the house.

Zeke shot up and hit a few buttons on the security system. The sirens stopped. "Sorry about that. Make sure you tell me when you need to go outside."

I rolled my eyes and entered the scary outdoors full of wild squirrels and children with squirt guns ready to take out an eye.

With the delay in Holbrook, we planned to spend the night at Zeke's house instead of a hotel before going to pick up Westward and Corbin at the airport the next evening. When I came through the front door, no one came to help, but at least the alarm didn't go off again. The boys sat and chatted like two old ladies who'd known each other for years. Tina reclined in a rocker in the corner, flipping through a magazine.

I put on my best, irritated voice. "Do you mind if I interrupt to ask where I'll be sleeping?"

"Oh, I'm sorry. Shay and I were just talking about some things we have in common." Zeke jumped up and grabbed the suitcase off the floor next to me. Shay didn't move a muscle.

"And what might that be? The material you used on the curtains in your kitchen or your fashion sense?" Although my question was a response to Zeke, I kept my eyes firmly set on Shay's.

"We were talking about teaching. Zeke and I both teach advanced level high school physics. But I guess you didn't know that about me, did you?" His words stung, but he was right, our careers usually stayed out of the forefront of our conversations.

The tension between Shay and I clearly made our host uncomfortable as he put down my suitcase and went to adjust a miniature elephant with a monkey on its back. "Let me get you drinks." The words tumbled out of his mouth as if he didn't know what else to say.

"You'll get used to it." Tina rocked back and forth, still looking at her magazine. "No need to get all uptight and spastic, Zeke. Once these two get their roll in the hay, we'll all get a little bit of peace around here."

Heat rushed to my cheeks, so I grabbed my suitcase and went to the stairs. "Never mind. I'm sure I can find it on my own."

The landing at the top of the stairs showed a bedroom to the left and to the right. A fire extinguisher casing, like the one in the hallway at school, was installed at the top of the stairs. The bedroom on the left had a bed, and even though it was immaculate, it appeared to be lived in, so I carried my luggage to the other bedroom. Two twin sized beds with patchwork quilts were against a pale pink wall. Beaded lampshades stood on nightstands on the far side of each bed. A cherry wood dresser with an antique mirror displayed unique picture frames with black and white pictures of relatives long since deceased. The polished wood floors were covered with a light green area rug that perfectly finished off the adorable room.

The doorbell rang as I unpacked one set of clothes and my pajamas into a dresser drawer. Two dormer windows overlooked the front of the house, so I peeked to the street below. Behind my Jeep was a van with *Flying Monkey Express* painted across the side. A ghastly picture of a monkey with huge white wings carrying a letter in his hand covered the back end of the vehicle.

I set my suitcase near the closet and flopped down on the bed to rest for a while. The day traveled through my mind like a horrible nightmare, but I finally blocked it out with a moment of sleep. I dreamt of home—my house, my bed, and the memories of growing up with my aunt and uncle. I dreamt of Corbin and having his strong arms around me, far from the danger of murderers. His embrace felt so real that the dream made me long for him. He stroked my back and nuzzled his face into my neck. But why didn't Corbin shave? He always shaved. I awoke to find Shay beside me on the bed with his arm on top of mine.

I sat up and frowned. "What are you doing here?"

"Is that anyway to greet the man of your dreams?" He ran his hand back down my arm. "You smiled in response to my touch. Were you dreaming of me?"

I jumped off the bed and headed for the door. "Seriously, Shay. What are you doing in here? There's already too much talk about us. You heard Tina."

"Oh, don't get your panties in a bunch, darling. You send out so many mixed signals, I'm surprised a couple of small planes haven't crashed in the area." He sat up and pulled an envelope out of his pocket. "This was sent to you express delivery."

"What is it?" I snatched the envelope out of his hand. The same hideous monkey from the van was printed on the back of the envelope. "Flying Monkey Express."

"Yeah, they just dropped it off, so it must be something important from home." Westward was the only one with Zeke's address. I could only imagine what the witch wanted now. Maybe she wanted me to have her black robes pressed and ironed before the big ball on Saturday night. Or perhaps she wanted me to double check on the hotel's pet policy so she could bring her black cat. I ripped open the envelope, knowing that whatever it contained wasn't good.

It was a flight schedule with a yellow sticky note attached. "Please make sure you are on time." Tossing the Westward-infested note into the trash, I scanned the schedule to make sure they were still arriving in the evening. Running my finger down the itinerary, the arrival time had been changed to ten o'clock tomorrow morning.

"Great." I handed the paper to Shay and collapsed onto the other bed. "This is her fault somehow. She just wants to make my life miserable."

Shay got up to lie next to me, the paper gone. "Don't let her get to you. So we get an early start. I don't like to run by a schedule, anyways. All we need is a little extra coffee."

His fingers laced into mine as I looked at him. "Physics, huh? I would've pictured you as a chemistry type of guy. They allow you to blow stuff up in that class."

"True, but my Uncle Bob was a physics professor at the college when I was a kid. He'd show me all the cool demonstrations he used with his students and let me play around. Give me something to do and I'm hooked."

"So why a teaching conference on differentiated instruction if you only teach the advanced placement kids?"

Shay shrugged his shoulders. "Because I can, and it's in Vegas. Last year the school sent me to Honolulu. Maybe next year I'll find something in London or Paris." He swept a stray hair out of my face, keeping his eyes on mine.

"Don't you ever want to settle down?"

"Do you?" My eyes wandered down to his neckline as I tried to reflect on his question. The top two buttons of his shirt were undone and my mind drifted back to our first night together.

"I'm not sure." I sat up, but kept his hand in mine. "It would be nice to have a family someday, but I want to have fun first."

"Then let's go out tonight." Shay grabbed my other hand and pulled me to my feet. "I want some time alone together before my competition shows up. I'm going to ask Zeke where to find the action."

I raised both eyebrows and chuckled. "I'm sure he'll say an interior decorators' expo or a neighborhood watch meeting." Zeke probably didn't nightclub. Too many germs.

"So you don't think he hangs with the ladies downtown?" I raised my eyebrows higher this time. "Let me check with him while you get dressed."

Shay hesitated at the door, and then turned back to me. He took my hands again, placing his forehead against mine. He kept his voice to a whisper. "And I promise not to take you to a gay bar this time."

"That's good to know." I gave him a push toward the door.

My thoughts were miles away from Shay's competition when I headed to the living room thirty minutes later. I paused halfway down the stairs, crouching like a child spying on Santa Claus. I spent a couple of minutes admiring him. He shaved his stubble, and his jaw line was fully exposed for the first time since I met him. His light brown hair fell slightly above his shoulders and was tousled in a free, sexy type of way. The light colored shirt he wore showed off his tanned skin with the top two buttons undone again. He wore a dark pair of wranglers, which I swear are the only brand men in Texas buy.

Shay and Zeke studied a map at the coffee table, but when I descended, they glanced up. My face beamed when I saw Shay's mouth drop, knowing that the blue summer dress I threw on was the right choice. Entering the living room, I noticed Tina for the first time sprawled out on the couch. She appeared to be extremely bored. Without thinking, I said, "Why don't you come with us?"

"Nah." She waved a hand at me. "You two kids have fun. Besides, Zeke's promised an exhilarating evening of Star Wars episodes and Parcheesi. He's also going to share his stamp collection with me if I'm good." Tina stood up and walked toward the kitchen, so I followed her leaving the two men to their map reading.

Safely out of earshot, I prodded Tina. "Zeke should come, too. I'm sure he's never been out at night. Maybe he'd enjoy it."

"No, we'll stay here." Tina poured a bowl of cereal. She really knew her way around for someone who'd only been here a couple of hours. "Shay would kill me if we came anyway."

"It's not a date, Tina." I gave her the most innocent face I could muster. "We're just going out to have some fun. Now don't tell me that you want to spend the evening with Luke Skywalker playing board games."

"I don't know, he's actually kind of cute in a dorky way. And we both know that I need to find a nice guy who has his life together." She shoved a spoonful of Rice Krispies into her mouth, making her next line harder to understand. "You can't have all of them."

"But don't throw yourself at the first guy that comes along that you think matches your description."

Tina looked down as I moved in closer.

"This guy sees a therapist and has serious issues with dirt."

"You're one to talk." She put down the bowl. "I think you've successfully thrown yourself and knocked down the one man that brings out your wilder side. Did you think about who you're hurting along the way? At least with Zeke, I only hurt myself."

"It's not like that with Shay." I kept a straight face. "We're friends."

"Now that's the biggest lie I've ever heard. The whole sheriff's department in Holbrook was talking about that kiss in the interrogation room. So, stop lying to me and don't you dare judge my relationships." Tina scooped up her bowl and left for the living room.

～い い〜

Shay drove into Flagstaff, leaving me drowning in Tina's accusations. He tried to start conversations about the conference or the time he surfed the biggest waves in Hawaii, but my mind kept blocking him out providing the necessary conventional answers and acknowledgements.

"So, am I going on a date with you tonight, or some lifeless robot that took over your body?" He grinned, but his eyes told me that he was waiting for an answer. Shay parked the car on the side of a busy street. The sidewalk teemed with pedestrians taking in the nightlife. A couple in their forties laughed and held hands, entering the bar outside my door.

I watched another couple come out the same door. "Do you ever wonder what life might be like twenty years from now?"

"No way. It might cause me to go into a state of severe depression." Reaching across the seat, Shay slipped his arm around my neck and pressed his lips to mine. "I tend to live for today."

He was right. That's the reason I came on this trip. To live for today. I needed to stop over thinking things and just let loose.

Shay took my hand and led me through the front door. Some country star sang a sappy song about his tractor as Shay swung me onto the dance floor leading me in the two-step.

"Did you ever wonder how a tractor's sexy?" Shay and I worked our way over to a corner table. Some woman now sang about her boots. "I mean there's nothing sexy about machinery that works in manure. Most of the guys that work tractors around Amarillo are balding and have a beer gut."

I sent him a sweet smile, taking in the scene around us and letting him ramble on.

He took off his cowboy hat, placing it on my head. "Now that's sexy."

The hours flashed by. I let my mindless state take over and I lived for the moment, maybe for the first time in my life. The blaring music, the beers, and the men who asked me to dance—the whole experience blurred into a country song about a girl who no longer knew herself. I was a zombie whose sole purpose was submerging myself in the depths of mindlessness. My realization came when I was dirty dancing with a hunk of a man named Buck. He was certainly nice on the eyes, but I didn't know him from a hole in the wall. My connection wasn't with the wild and reckless, it was with …

"Do you mind if I cut in?" Shay had his hand on my arm, tapping Buck with his finger.

"Actually, I do." Buck whipped me around so my arm was ripped free from Shay's hand. "I don't see your name on her." With those words, I wrenched myself free from the slave master.

"The tattoo shop a couple of doors down closes at three." Shay moved around Buck toward me. "So I thought my name would look perfect in some type of flowery script right about here." He pushed back my hair and kissed me on my neck sending a pleasant chill down my spine.

Buck grabbed my hand and yanked me away from Shay again, clutching me against his chest in a way that had me regretting not taking those self-defense classes offered at the community center last year. Although, I did have one trick up my pant leg. Turning toward Buck, I placed my arms around his neck, luring the fly into my web. When my lips met his, I heard Shay grunt behind me. Buck's kiss became more forceful, but I had him exactly where I wanted him. With one swift soccer-style knee to the groin, I had him collasping to the floor in pain.

"Remind me to always stay on your good side." Shay touched my arm. "When I saw him grab you like that, I was ready to knock him out."

"That's why I took matters into my own hands," I said approaching the Jeep. "You need to use a little more of your brain and a little less of your testosterone."

"Now about that tattoo." He brushed my neck with his fingertips again.

"You're using your testosterone again. Do I need to knee some sense into you, too?" The engine sputtered when I turned the key, but with a couple of revs, it roared to life.

"Tempting, but no."

I was relieved that I was going home with someone like him and not someone like Buck. After an hour of wrong turns and asking for directions, I pulled the Jeep into the fortress. No sirens went off when I unlocked the front door with the key that Zeke had given me. Tina and Zeke were fast asleep on the two couches in the front room. Some science fiction movie flickered across the television screen. Shay turned off the television, then took my hand and led me upstairs to the spare bedroom.

Closing the door, he whispered, "I know we have to get up in a couple of hours, so maybe it'd be better if we slept in separate beds." Shay crossed the room and enveloped me in his arms, both of us refusing to let go.

"Tomorrow's going to change things. And it's not just Corbin. She'll be there and I know she'll find some way to ruin this."

His embrace loosened as he led me to one of the beds, lying down and pulling me to his chest. "Nothing could ruin what we have. You're one of the most amazing people I've met in my life."

His chest rose and fell erratically, and at that moment I wanted him—and it wasn't just the alcohol speaking. It was as if I could change myself into a free spirit through osmosis. The closer I could get to him, the freer I would be. I turned my body to face his, finding his mouth within seconds. His lips were experienced, kissing my jaw line, my neck, the lobe of my ear. The heat rushed through my body in anticipation. Lifting me to a sitting position, he found the buttons on the front of my dress, quickly revealing the white lace of my bra. He helped me lift his shirt over his head. I covered his chest with light kisses before bringing my lips to his jaw line and then again to his mouth. Shay groaned with wanting as I undid the buttons to his jeans. He removed my last pieces of clothing before we melded together, two free spirits choosing to spend one night of our lives together. We fell asleep in each other's arms, trying not to dream of what tomorrow would bring.

Chapter 12

A knock came on the door long before I was ready to get up. Shay's arm moved as I lifted my head from the small puddle of drool my mouth deposited on the pillow. Still undressed from the night before, I stumbled to the bathroom with a pair of jeans and a long-sleeved shirt. Through some miraculous act, the four of us were in the Jeep and hitting the road by five o'clock. I agreed to let Zeke drive while I rode shotgun, giving Tina and Shay some extra shuteye in the back. As we passed the city limits my eyes began to droop, so I stuck Toto into the tape player.

With our early start I was sure we'd arrive on time for our ten o'clock pickup at the airport. I stared out my window as first morning's light filtered across the landscape, turning the indecipherable shadows into trees, rocks, and houses. A sudden, sobbing noise beside me caught my attention. Zeke's face was covered with tears—his eyes red, his chest heaving.

I opened the glove box to find a tissue and handed it to him. "What's wrong, Zeke? Do you need me to drive?"

He blew his nose in a loud sort of way, like Uncle Embry during allergy season. I glanced back at the other two passengers, but they were still sound asleep. "You'd think you'd never see a big guy like me cry like a frickin' baby."

"Can't say it's something I see every day." I always try to be honest. "But it doesn't mean you can't do it." I handed him another tissue and a plastic bag to throw his trash in.

Zeke bit his lip, physically in pain from trying to hold back the tears. "It's the song."

"Toto made you upset?" The pure insanity of the thought made me bite my lip in wonder.

"My last girlfriend's name was Rosanna." He turned the Jeep onto another road that headed north. It was a good thing that one of us was paying attention.

"So you had a hard time with the break-up?"

"That was the best part. She ran with the girls in the roller derby, you know, the ones with the unnaturally big muscles. Well, I don't think she ever liked me. She just needed a punching bag to work out her frustrations, and I never fought back. I could never hit a girl. I didn't have the guts to tell her to get the hell out of my house. I was too afraid of her."

"I'm sorry, Zeke."

"Imagine … a mountain of a man like me afraid of a girl. What kind of man am I?"

I folded up the map, unsure of how to respond because I lacked empathy—being a petite woman.

We rode through a tiny town with a rundown gas station, a collecting ground for tumbleweeds. "Maybe you need to make this time a spiritual renewal," I said, unsure of Zeke's religious background.

"My therapist can't help me. How can God help me?" He forced a weak smile in my direction.

"Hey, anything can happen in Vegas. Who knows? Maybe you'll meet the girl of your dreams. One that won't take advantage of you." I glanced back at Shay, momentarily. "For some reason I feel like this trip will hold a lot of answers for all of us."

"What's Tina's story?" Zeke kept his eyes on the road. I knew it took a lot of courage for him to ask me that question.

"She's a lost soul looking for a place to belong," I said, confident in my answer. "You'd better be careful though. Tina's broken hundreds of hearts in the greater Albuquerque area without an ounce of guilt attached."

"We had a good time last night. She's a huge Star Wars fan."

"You've got to be kidding." I laughed, trying to think of Tina with Princess Leia buns in her hair.

"No, for real. And it's not like she watches it because she thinks Anakin Skywalker's hot. She knows stuff. She told me the name of every Sith lord. Even the ones in the books."

"Wow, maybe one of the casinos will have a Star Wars convention we can sign her up for so she won't feel left out while we're gone during the day."

"She's deeper than you think, Dottie." Zeke seemed to go into defensive mode.

"Well then … why don't you ask her out?"

Zeke rolled his eyes. "Isn't it obvious?" He tapped his fingers on the steering wheel in some kind of erratic melody. "No. No way. She's got to ask me."

"What's the worse she can do? Say no?" The task didn't seem so difficult to me. If you liked somebody, you had to let them know. My problem was I had two somebodies.

"Yes. She'd crush me. I'm too afraid of that." Zeke whispered with the sound of stirring in the backseat. Shay placed his chin on the back of my seat, touching my hair with his lips and alerting me to our surroundings.

A huge white dam blocked a river in the gorge ahead of us. Cars slowed to take in the immensity of the structure. I'd seen pictures of the Hoover Dam in a history book Uncle Embry kept among the books he studied on his shelf in the living room. A large sign welcoming us to Nevada grew out of the rocks on the far side.

I pulled my shoebox from under the passenger seat. "Can you park on the other side of the dam?"

Zeke nodded. "Sounds good. I'd like to stretch my legs, too."

Stepping out onto the gravel parking lot, I went straight for the walkway that crossed the dam. I didn't wait for the others. About halfway across, I stopped and peeked over the side. It must've been holding back millions of tons of water, just like my heart held back the years of hurt Corbin caused me. I hid the hurt behind my ability to hold it together in a town where everyone knew our secret. And I always thought that if I could just break that dam holding back the hurt everything would be alright. Maybe sleeping with Shay would hurt Corbin as much as he hurt me, but now I wasn't so sure.

Corbin's letter. He didn't profess his love in his words. He didn't apologize for never telling me the truth. But for some reason, looking at his handwriting that had grown from a sloppy cursive script from when he was twelve to an even sloppier printed script as an adult, I wanted to put his note back in my pocket instead of sending it over the edge as a kamikaze airplane.

⌁

At nine o'clock, the tall buildings of the Vegas strip appeared before us with a billboard every eighth of a mile advertising a steak breakfast for a buck ninety-nine or a topless extravaganza. Shay drove into the downtown area while I rode in the passenger seat. Zeke was as close to his door as he could get, trying desperately to avoid any physical contact with Tina. She was just beside herself with excitement. With her window rolled down, she whistled at any young guy that happened to be in whistling distance. Poor Zeke.

We pulled up to the front entrance of the Emerald City Hotel and Casino, the largest hotel that I'd ever seen. A gigantic screen attached to the front of the building flashed messages announcing the arrival of the teachers' conference. A bellboy dressed in a green suit and tuxedo tails offered to take the bags that Shay and Zeke unloaded, but my companions declined any help.

I jingled my keys between my fingers as I waited by the driver's side door. Zeke carried all of Tina's bags up the stairs into the hotel lobby.

Shay had his backpack on his shoulder when he came to the front of the Jeep. "I'll just take your bags up to my room and you can come get them when you get back." With his hands stuck in the pockets of his jeans, he appeared nervous, like he knew something ominous was on the horizon. "Are you sure you don't want me to go with you?"

The idea was tempting. I'd basically be shouting my proclamation of a new life in Corbin's face, but deep down I wasn't ready. "I'm sure." I tried to keep the mood light. "Don't go bungee jumping off the Stratosphere while I'm gone. If you're doing that, you're taking me with you."

"Wouldn't even think of it. I need you to do all the fun stuff now. You know, going to gay bars, getting arrested. I think I might even need you to truck surf." He pulled me into an embrace. "I hear it's a hundred times better bungee jumping with someone else. If you're kissing someone on the way down you're far less likely to get a mouth full of bugs."

I reached for the handle of the door, knowing the clock was ticking with Westward. "I'll remember that." Shay pulled me back from the car and kissed me like he did at the sheriff's office, urgent and passionate. Maybe he thought if he could kiss me hard enough, he'd hold onto me, but at the moment I didn't care. I was lost in the feeling of his lips. They found my neck, my collarbone, coming around to my lips again. When would this desperate attraction that I felt for him stop?

Then he was gone and I was by myself for the first time since Saturday morning. The airport was only a ten-minute drive, so I parked the Jeep, and hunted down the arrival gate with several minutes to spare. With my low maintenance morning still apparent on my face, I went to the bathroom to brush my hair and apply make-up. No one else was in the bathroom, so I lifted my arms to smell my pits. What I wouldn't give for a shower right now.

Westward's red hair was the first thing that caught my attention when the next group of travelers wandered out of the concourse. A mix-matched group, the professionals zoomed ahead, knowing precisely where they were going—taking out any confused tourists in their way. Westward fell in between the two groups. She had no idea where she was going, but she sure wasn't going to let anyone know. Corbin carried her carry-on trying to keep up with her pacing.

"Corbin!" I waved my hand above the crowd. He nodded at me and then grabbed Westward's elbow as she started to head in the wrong direction. She greeted me with her usual grimace.

"You'd think a teacher would have the foresight to rent a cart for the luggage," Westward grumbled, hauling off toward the baggage claim.

"Nice to see you too, Maxine."

"Well, I'm happy to see you. Does that count?" Corbin set down Westward's giraffe print carry-on, wrapping me in his arms. He smelled of Kansas, earthy and fresh, jumbled together with burgers from the Dive. I missed that smell.

Westward's voice snapped across the concourse. "Don't put down my luggage, Mr. Lane. Someone might try to confiscate it." The acrimonious tone in her voice caused numerous eyes to evaluate Westward and then the object of her comments. They drifted back, one by one, into their own lives once they realized that an imminent gladiatorial battle was not likely between the two foes.

"See what I've had to deal with?" Corbin reached down to pick up the case. "I thought the flight attendant was going to throw her out the emergency exit."

The ride to the hotel was filled with Westward's goals for the conference. Corbin drove, while I laid in the backseat trying to block her incessant barking out of my head.

"And Dottie, you and I will stay together on the ninth floor." Waking me from my daydreams, her words hit me, each word a brick against the side of my head. Corbin caught my horror through the rearview mirror.

"Maxine, I'll arrange for Dottie to have her own room. I'm sure after a long day at the conference it'll be preferable for both of you." He kept his voice calm, trying to sooth her with his words.

"If that's the way you want it, Mr. Lane." Westward faced me in the backseat. "I want you to know that you are holding up the reputation of our school with your conduct here in Las Vegas."

"I'll try not to stand on the street corner in my lingerie." I put on the smile that I reserved just for her. Maybe I'd do it just to spite her.

"That's good to hear, since I'm sure very few would like to see that—myself included."

Corbin raised his eyebrows in the rearview mirror, and I wondered if he conjured up the image in his head.

Westward had a small zoo's worth of luggage caged up in the back of my Jeep, so Corbin and I helped her lug it to the front desk. A petite woman with a green suit checked in Westward first, taking her credit card information. I glanced into the immense lobby. The middle stretched above me, endless floors of opulence. Everything was emerald green, but tasteful, not tacky. Cocktail waitresses carried drinks dressed in very short blue and white checkered dresses, two pigtails in each woman's hair.

While Westward went on and on about the amenities she expected in her hotel room, Shay stepped off the elevator at the other side of the casino floor. I stood behind Corbin, mustering the maturity of a second grader as I peeked around him. This was not the time to introduce Corbin to Shay. The conversation I pictured in my head many times already reminded me of a bad sitcom. "Corbin, this is Shay. You two should hang out sometime because you have so much in common. Corbin, you want to sleep with me and Shay already has. Now you have loads to talk about."

"What are you doing, Dottie?" Corbin peered over his shoulder to find me glued to his back.

"Just waiting my turn." I glanced in Shay's direction. He sat at a blackjack table with a stack of chips. This settled my nerves a bit as Westward stepped aside and I handed the desk clerk my license and credit card.

A loud siren blasted and a multitude of colored balloons and confetti fell around us, drawing the attention of the entire ground floor of the casino. Hundreds of eyes tore away from the monotony of the slots to look directly at me as a spotlight lit me up like a Christmas tree. My cheeks glowed hot as I shrugged my shoulders, managing to lift a hand to wave to the sea of people.

"The Emerald City Hotel and Casino would like to congratulate Dottie Gale, winner of our millionth customer give away!" The voice boomed over the racket of the slot machines, but the heat continued to rush to my cheeks when Shay's eyes met mine. So much for going undercover.

A white-haired man in a tuxedo and three scantily dressed women in brightly colored costumes approached me. Brandishing an envelope and more balloons, he bowed. "How do you feel right now, Ms. Gale? I'm sure you're elated beyond words!"

I squinted in the spotlight's glare. "If you knew me, you'd know that I'm never really speechless. But to tell you the truth, Mr…?" Lights flashed around us and a crowd began to gather in the lobby area. My eyes searched for Shay among the onlookers.

"Uh, Mr. Oswald. I'm the owner of the casino." His back straightened, a proud father to a gluttonous child.

"Mr. Oswald, I'm not exactly sure what I've won. I'm just here to attend the teachers' conference for my school back in Kansas."

"Then we couldn't have picked someone more worthy. Your face will be plastered on every square inch of the casino. Nothing but the red carpet for you, Ms. Gale. You've won the use of the penthouse suite for the entire length of your stay."

"Can I give my prize away?" I considered how Westward would make my life a living hell if I didn't offer the suite to her.

"Now that's a horse of a different color." Mr. Oswald laughed. "A generous soul in Las Vegas. No, you can't give your prize away, but the suite is yours. Your friends are welcome to stay with you." Mr. Oswald spoke to the desk clerk, then handed me the key to my room. "This key will work the elevator, your door lock, and the fully stocked refrigerator in the room. All complementary."

My senses were so over stimulated that I never noticed Westward creeping in on the conversation. "Perfect! This is just perfect, Mr. Oswald!" She put on as much charm as she could throw at him. "Dottie is an employee that I hold in the highest regard. We were just discussing our room assignments. It would be like a sleepover. Just us girls." She squeezed my shoulder as I fought to control my gag reflex.

"Thank you, Mr. Oswald." I lowered my voice as much as possible in the noisy room, trying to block out Westward. "Can I ask you one more favor?"

"If it's in my power." His voice was hushed.

"Do you think you and the girls could escort me to the elevator? I'm trying to avoid someone." Glancing over my shoulder at Westward, I added, "Actually two people."

Oswald linked arms with me and we glided across the lobby, a waning crowd following behind us. The hotel's glass elevator was the centerpiece of the atrium, shooting up to the multiple floors above our heads. Mr. Oswald stepped into the elevator, showing me how to use the key to get to the penthouse. Corbin and Westward stood right outside the elevator. Westward's face appeared as if it might explode.

More to spite her than anything else, I said, "Are you coming, Mr. Lane?"

Corbin grinned from ear to ear and quickly crossed the threshold. The elevator raced upward without a stop because its destination was usually reserved for the rich and famous. Corbin grabbed my hand at the same moment I spotted Shay next to the tropical foliage surrounding the wishing fountain. He wasn't looking at me anymore, but tossed a coin into the water while he turned to walk away.

Chapter 13

"Oh, my stars! Can you believe this Corb?" I felt the urge to run through the suite taking in everything at once, but my shock kept me planted in the entrance hallway. Two huge pillars reached up to the massive ceiling intricately painted to resemble the sky on the most perfect night. In the center of the room, a Roman statue of a naked man with a jar poured water into a small swimming pool. "Now I know we're not in Kansas anymore. They don't make stuff like this where we're from."

Corbin laughed. "I don't think they make stuff like this in Oklahoma City."

The rest of the suite delivered luxury upon luxury. A gigantic flat screen television descended from the ceiling with a touch of a button. Gas log fireplaces adorned the living room and bedroom. The ornate antique furniture and oriental vases worth more than my entire house. I opened the refrigerator with my room key and found it stocked with every food I could imagine—and some I couldn't.

The four-poster canopy bed was covered with a deep red satin bedspread and a barrage of pillows, reminding me of a princess's quarters I once saw in a Grimm's fairytale book. Running from the doorway to the bedroom, I sailed through the air onto the bed, sinking deep into the lush bedding. "Will you fire me if I decide to stay in bed instead of going to the conference?"

Corbin settled onto the edge of the mattress, using more conventional means, lying next to me like we did that night in his apartment. He turned his head toward me, his blue eyes as endless as ever. "Will you ever forgive me?"

"How can I forgive you for something you never did?" I ran my fingers through the dark hairs that fell into his face. My eyes wandered from his eyes to his lips, full and perfect. Those lips hadn't touched mine in almost seven years, but they were patient, waiting until I was ready. "Wanda told me what happened before I left. I know you didn't lie to me."

Corbin propped his head up on his elbow, taking in my face as his body pitched precariously in my direction. The image of Shay tossing the coin into the fountain filled my mind. Unlike Tina, I'm not the type of girl that goes around kissing every guy that shows an interest.

I floundered for an excuse to get off the bed. "Um … I've got to call Westward." My heart beat rapidly, so I took a deep breath trying to suppress something I'd denied for years.

"Why in the hell do you have to do that?" Corbin was clearly angry by Corbin standards.

"I want to make sure she made it to her room alright without our help." I picked up the phone. As the front desk connected me to Westward's room, Corbin grabbed his jacket and stormed to the front door.

It closed with a slam as Westward answered. "You'd better watch yourself, you little tramp." She was a natural when it came to degrading jargon. "You might have Corbin Lane fooled, but you can't fool me."

"Maxine, I'm only calling to see if you're happy with your room." I sighed. I absentmindedly picked up the pen next to the phone and doodled Corbin's name scribbling a tiny heart above the *i* like I did when I was fifteen.

"Let's see, I hate the whole Wizard of Oz themed décor, the bedding is old, the shower has splotches of mold, and the staff left plain old mints instead of Andes on my pillow. Do I need to say more?" A loud click came from the other end, leaving me listening to a dial tone.

Since I already managed to tick off two people, I thought that perhaps the third time would be a charm. The front desk gave me Shay's room number on the third floor, so I rode the elevator down to retrieve my suitcase. I knocked four times before he answered, and his puffy eyes told me he'd been sleeping. That, and the fact that boxer shorts were the only thing he had on.

"I thought you'd never come." He opened the door wider to let me in. The room was dark with only a thin sliver of light reaching through the crack of the curtain.

"Yeah, you look like it's kept you up for hours." I glanced around, finding my bag in the hallway next to the bathroom. "You're not mad?"

"Only if you're leaving already." Shay blocked the hallway. "You didn't even tell me how it went with Westward and Pretty Boy. I mean, I know about the whole Dottie Gale extravaganza. Can't wait to see your posters everywhere, like on the wall when I'm playing poker or in the lobby bathroom when I'm taking a piss."

"Fine." I waited for him to release me and ignored his latter comments. "They made it safely. They found their rooms."

"That's not what I meant." Shay leaned his head against the wall. "Is he staying with you? I saw the two of you go up to the suite together."

"No, and stop being so jealous." I let the aggravation slip out. I hated sounding huffy and puffy, especially in my new orange lifestyle. "Everything's really complicated right now."

"Then I want my time." Shay reached out to me, not seeming to care about complications. "Don't go back to the suite for a while. You can rest here. You've got to be tired after last night." A small smile parted his lips. I felt like a child of parents with dual custody. The elevator ride to the penthouse seemed like an eternity to my aching head. Shay's bed, with its Emerald City covers, called out to me. Exhaustion swallowed me up as I stretched my body across it's green expanse. Some level of my subconscious was vaguely aware when Shay lifted the covers on the other side of the bed, his body moving close to mine. Then I drifted off.

Somewhere between the conscious and the subconscious is a place where your true desires are known. These desires are found in your dreams. In my dream, I woke up next to Corbin in my bedroom at home. A princess cut diamond ring graced my finger, the wedding plans spread across the kitchen table setting out the impending nuptials. Corbin was in the shower getting ready for work, when a knock came on the window. Shay peered in. I opened the window, inviting him into my bed. His lips covered my body, trying to kiss away the scent of Corbin. I giggled with his touch, igniting a flame within me. At the height of our forbidden ecstasy, the bathroom door opened, exposing our secret. He didn't yell, he didn't swear, he didn't hit Shay, he just left the room. But the look on his face killed me inside. It wasn't disappointment. It wasn't anger. It revealed a deadness where love used to be.

When I woke up, I was sweating. Shay still slept, trying to recover from the night before. I slipped out of bed and pulled aside the curtains catching a glimpse of the neon colors of Las Vegas Boulevard at night.

A few minutes later, Shay came up behind me and pulled me to him, away from the curtains and the life teeming out on the streets. "Spend time with him tonight," he whispered. "You've got some unresolved feelings."

"No." Standing on my toes, I pulled Shay's lips to mine. They were warm and filled with an inviting desire. "I'm with you."

～～～

My penthouse suite was more of a curse than a blessing as I wheeled my suitcase into the entrance hall. The larger the space, the emptier it felt when you were all alone, and right now my suite seemed to encompass all of Las Vegas.

A light blinked on my telephone, so I pushed all sorts of buttons trying to retrieve the call. I jumped back when a voice started blaring out of the machine at an ear-piercing decibel. I managed to turn it down slightly before the end of Tina's message. "Hey Dottie! Where've you been? Thought maybe we could all go out tonight. Give me a call in room 5264."

When Tina found out I was crashing in the penthouse suite, she was at my door in less than five minutes. The two of us primped in front of the sinks in my gigantic bathroom. Tina found a way to work my surround sound, so loud music filled the suite. Spaghetti straps held up my short yellow dress as it hugged the curves and contours of my body, my legs accentuated by my heels. My long blonde hair, slightly curled on the ends, swished freely as I turned to look at my backside.

"They're going to be fighting over you." Tina smiled from her side of the vanity. She was wearing a jean skirt, a red tank top, and leather boots up to her knees.

"Shay and I are together." I sent her a look that told her to end the subject, even though my stomach flip-flopped. I still couldn't erase the fact that Corbin never cheated. It changed the whole dynamics of my hatred for him, for Quandary. How could I face him, with that wall demolished between us, and deny that I had feelings for him? Strong feelings. I had to get Corbin Lane out of my head. "Did you know that Zeke's got a thing for you?"

"He's, well, he's … just being nice." She touched up her lipstick, glancing at me out of the corner of her eye. "Do you really think so?"

"He's not going to make the first move." I applied a round of pink gloss. "You better use those little powers of yours." I gathered the assorted make-up into my bag. "And don't you dare break his heart."

~~~

When Tina and I stepped into the elevator, my heart began to pound in harmony with my flipping stomach. I knew there was no turning back, but I couldn't help but wonder if my relationship with Shay would be immediately apparent to Corbin. I watched the numbers above our heads slowly descend, trying to keep my eyes from the lobby outside the glass walls. Inevitably, the L lit up and the doors opened. Tina skipped out, racing toward Zeke and Shay at the couches. Across the lobby, Corbin read a newspaper. Of course, Shay didn't invite him over. Even though Corbin apologized for his behavior in my room when I invited him to dinner, I wondered if he was still angry. There's no turning back, I told myself again.

I kept my eyes on Corbin, even though Shay's eyes were on me, and the whole time I should have kept my eyes on the multi-leveled floor below me. My heel caught on a step leading up to the area where Corbin sat. He looked up from the newspaper just as I stumbled forward and into the lap of a stranger. Corbin was there by my side, and several moments later, Shay was there, suppressing a smile.

"Are you alright?" Corbin took my hand. His familiar eyes held nothing but concern.

"I'd give that fall a 9.6." Shay unleashed his smile from its suppression, his hand on my knee.

The man that was so kind to cushion my fall shot a toothless grin at me. Oxygen tubes wrapped from his nose and around his ears. He took off his fedora and placed it over his heart. "I have to say, miss. I've just arrived here, and already this place is living up to my expectations."

Shay took my hands. "Let me help you up so this man can breathe again."

"I don't think we've met." Corbin sized up Shay as a possible adversary. He stood up straighter, sticking out his hand.

"Shay Fields." He shook Corbin's hand. "Dottie was kind enough to pick me up on her way to Vegas." Shay's *anything goes* personality was thrown to the wayside as his arm slipped around my waist and he took on a territorial stance. He kissed my hair, causing my comfort level to plummet to the basement below. My eyes looked everywhere, except at Corbin's face.

"I thought you were traveling alone." Corbin was clearly hurt by Shay's public display of affection. I slipped out of Shay's arm, trying to paint the illusion of friendship in his gesture.

"Westward made me pick up a couple of teachers along the way to save the school money." Tina and Zeke came up the stairs behind Shay.

"Yep, she's a hell of a girl, Corbin. Picked up these two for the school and took on a freeloader like me." As Tina's eyes took in Corbin, I felt my own territorial side kick in.

I linked my arm in his. "Corbin Lane, this is Tina Steele and Zeke Lyons. Zeke teaches high school physics in Flagstaff, and Tina is keeping her occupational options open here in Vegas."

The four shook hands before we went downstairs to the casino's swanky restaurant, The Dungeon. The rich people in Quandary drove their oversized pick-up trucks to Chuck's Chop House on Saturday night for a large slab of meat and a baked potato. Apparently, in Las Vegas, high-class included manacles, gargoyles, and gothic imagery. Strobe lights flashed from a dance floor in the center of the restaurant, where the young and attractive kept their bodies moving in perfect beat with the music.

The hostess found our reservation and led us to our table that was located in one of the many dungeon cells that lined the walls.

"Didn't think we'd end up here again." Shay shouted above the music. "Well, at least not until I'd had a few drinks."

When we sat down in our ornate chairs, the music became more tolerable. Shay and Corbin took the seats on either side of me, and it became painfully obvious that they weren't talking. Ignoring them, I propped my menu in front of me and tried to decide between the crystal ball of pasta or the filet of flying monkey.

After a few minutes, I set my menu down after settling on the pasta, gripping the edges of my chair. "So, Mr. Oswald handed me four spa certificates for Saturday. A couple of hours of pampering might be just what I need."

Tina squealed. "I've never been to a spa. Do you think it'd be like the ones they have on the soap operas on the T.V? My cousin Nicky has always done my hair and nails."

Corbin's hand reached down and found mine on the edge of the chair, so I shot him a sidelong smile. His physical innuendos had certainly multiplied over the past week. The emotional clues were always there, but other than a professional handshake, he hadn't touched me since the incident with Wanda Jo.

"Why don't you take your three friends?" Corbin stroked the side of my hand. Guilt flared up in me with Shay to my left. "I'm sure you could use it after your trip."

"I don't need a spa." Shay ran his fingers through his hair before putting his cowboy hat back on. "I'm no stinkin' metrosexual like Pretty Boy over here."

"Did someone mention our spa treatments?" Westward stood at the door of the suddenly stifling cell, one hand on the doorframe, the other on her hip. Her short, black dress was strapless and leather, too young for sagging triceps and stomach rolls. A hideous tiger shawl clung to her shoulders, making me wonder if one of the poor creatures down the street at the Mirage fell into her clutches. Westward looked right at me. "I didn't receive your phone call for dinner. I must've been in the shower."

Corbin stood up and pulled out the chair next to him like he was dining with a lady instead of a monster. Westward sat down and turned her attention to the other three at the table. "Maxine Westward. I don't believe you've had the pleasure of my acquaintance."

Zeke had his eyes on something intensely interesting under the table. Tina pursed her lips together. It must've been the first time she met someone with a head as big as her own. Shay rose, reaching his hand across the table. "I'm Shay Fields."

"My, my, Mr. Fields." Maxine held onto his hand a little longer than necessary. "Dottie's been keeping you from us. She didn't tell me how attractive you were."

My face flushed as I thought about how she was old enough to be his mother. Maybe this was her ploy to drive a wedge into my friendship with Corbin. Either way, she deserved an icy stare.

"I like a woman who appreciates the finer things in life," Shay said, still standing. "Would you like to dance, Ms. Westward?"

"I'd love to, Mr. Fields, but please call me Maxine." She blushed and stood up to take his hand. Yuck! Double yuck! As they left the cell, Shay sent me a wink over his shoulder before strolling away to slow dance with the enemy.

"That's one nasty woman." Zeke glanced over at the dance floor. "How do you two put up with her? If she were my boss, I'd be teaching on-line, not cooped up in a school where I'd have to see her day in and day out."

"Only the tough survive, Zeke." I thought of Sue Fox. "We're waiting for the next twister to carry her away—or us away. It's got to be one or the other."

Corbin chuckled beside me. "So that's the way it's got to be, Dot? Either she goes or you go?" He took my hand again, this time pulling me up toward the dance floor. Over the blaring music he shouted. "Are you planning your escape on this trip?"

Corbin spun me around before I could answer, and then I was back in his arms, our hips swaying in unison. This was our first time dancing together since the prom, and it felt right being so close to him, but I knew I couldn't let my feelings for him get in the way of my plans. There was no turning back.

"Shay seems like a nice guy."

The comment woke me from my trance and I shook off the distractions in my head. "Come up to my room tonight." I knew I had to tell him the truth. I had to douse the fire before my old feelings for Corbin flared up. "We need to talk."

Zeke never pulled together the courage to ask Tina out to the dance floor, so he sat at the table enduring her endless chattering. Shay and Westward arrived shortly after we sat down, followed by our food—which was delivered by our prison guard. For the most part, the rest of dinner went well. I tolerated Westward's presence when her mouth was full of mashed potatoes. Halfway through the meal, Shay's hand found my thigh. He ate the rest of his Scarecrow's Harvest left-handed.

"So Mr. Fields said that the four of you had quite an adventure on the way out here." Westward cut her chicken with a knife. "I didn't know you were so naughty, Dottie."

I picked up my napkin to hide my blush, wondering what Shay told Westward while they danced. "Nothing you wouldn't have done, Maxine."

"Oh, no, no." Westward laughed while picking up her wine glass. "Incarceration, theft, hitch-hiking, fornication—and a little bit of littering thrown in on top of that."

Shay squeezed my thigh and shook his head at the twisting of his words, making us sound like a modern-day Bonnie and Clyde. My multiple warnings of her evil ways were not enough to keep Shay from being charmed by her glowing personality.

"Well, you know the saying, Maxine," I said. "What happens in Vegas … "

"Yeah, yeah, I know. Stays in Vegas." She munched a chunk of lettuce. "But I'm not sure if that saying applies in the other states you drove through. Maybe they need new slogans for their tourism campaigns. 'Have more sex in Texas.' Has a certain ring to it, doesn't it?" Westward's eyes wandered to Shay's arm, and I knew that she was on to our relationship.

My bottom remained planted in my seat even though I desired nothing more than to run away from Westward's twisting truths. I kept my eyes on my noodles, refusing to look at Corbin's face—which I'm sure was full of hurt and disappointment. It wasn't as bad as Westward made it out to be, but I was hiding parts of my relationship with Shay from Corbin. And I knew the game playing couldn't last much longer.

Chapter 14

On the way back to the elevator, I fell in love. Which man won? Ah, if only that decision were this simple. Instead, dazzlingly sleek lines on ruby red metal drew me to the Emerald City slot machines, where a glimmering Mustang convertible was on display. Surrounded by one-armed bandits, onlookers had full access to drool over the beautiful car. I rummaged through my purse and plucked out a ten-dollar bill to throw into the machine, certain to make me the instant winner of the sweet ride. I kissed the bill before pushing it into the money-feed, knowing luck had to be on my side.

My ten dollars rapidly turned into five as I glanced around the room for a familiar face. The others decided to try their luck in the casino, but I declined, wanting to get to bed early before my first class at nine the next morning. The luscious red convertible was merely a four-minute speed bump that kept me from my princess bed.

After Westward's proclamation of promiscuity, I didn't expect Corbin to come up to the suite, so I jumped in the shower to relax. She had pretty much laid the whole situation in front of his nose in black and white. What else did I have to tell him? That it was a mistake. That I didn't mean to sleep with Shay? But that would be a lie.

The knock sounded like it might be on the door to another room because the suite was so large, but

I slipped on my robe to check. I glanced through the peephole and sighed, not wanting to deal with the witch anymore tonight.

"Hi Maxine." I yawned to give her a hint, which she brushed aside as quickly as she brushed past me into the suite. "Did you come up to tell me that you won ten thousand dollars on a penny machine and want to split the winnings with me?"

"Enough of the shit, Dottie." Maxine grumbled, heading toward the kitchen. "Don't they stock this place with hard liquor?" She rummaged through the cabinets and I let her search for the non-existent liquids.

"I want to get to bed." I yawned and made my way toward the bedroom. "We've got an early morning, so I'll see you tomorrow. Feel free to crash on the couch."

"You're not going anywhere until I let you know how things are going to run around here." She sat down on the sofa, apparently giving up on the alcohol. I made a mental note to ask housekeeping to disinfect that spot on the couch.

I settled into the loveseat opposite her. My Uncle Embry used to call this kind of lecture an aspirin talk. Our medicine cabinet was fully loaded for the lectures Aunt Henrietta dished out on a regular basis.

"I'm having a party on Saturday night and I want to use the penthouse to entertain my guests." She looked around the massive suite, nodding at its decorations, but then glared right back at me. "It's a birthday party, so I want this place decked out … balloons, streamers, gigantic cake, and as much liquor as you can squeeze into that fridge of yours." She lifted herself from the sofa and walked around the room imagining her party decorations. "I think an ice sculpture of John would be perfect right about here."

"A what?!" I shook my head. "Where in the world are you going to get an ice sculpture? And who the hell is John?" I know most people don't talk to their bosses this way, but I think we both dropped the niceties and brandished the boxing gloves as soon as she threw my love life into the center of our restaurant table.

"We're in Vegas, Gale, not Kansas. They do the ice sculpture thing all the time here." She held out a curtain to examine the material. "And the party is for John Mellencamp, of course. Didn't you know it was his birthday?"

"No, I don't keep his birthday marked on my calendar." I thought about the horror of attending her delusional soirée. "The dance is that night, so don't even think about inviting me."

"Oh, I wouldn't dream about it." She ran her finger along a side table, examining it and nodding. "You'd never be on my guest list, but I do need a server for hors' oeuvres and cocktails. Just wear one of your swanky little outfits."

"Sorry, Maxine." I stood up and went to rest my head against the doorframe to the bedroom longing for one of Embry's aspirins. "I don't care if you use the penthouse, but I'm going to the dance."

"No." She flashed a wicked smile. "You'll be serving at my party, or I'll be letting Mr. Lane know about your relationship with Shay."

"And what makes you think I care if he knows? It's not like we're dating or anything. Technically, he's just my boss."

"And technically, you slept with another man. The only reason Corbin picked your name for this conference was to get back together with you. And I can tell by the way you look at him that you'd want nothing more than just that."

"But you made my relationship with Shay perfectly clear at dinner." I was ready to call security.

"He's a man, Dottie. He's clueless. But I can spell it out for him in black and white. Shay told me he is very fond of you, and you … *reciprocated* his affection, so to say."

"Then clearly I didn't warn him enough about you. And if you think that your blackmail attempts will work with me, then you obviously don't know who you're dealing with." This woman really was something else. She was reading between the lines and then some—and she didn't know when to stop.

"Yes, I do. But that's beside the point. You will serve at my party. You will find time to decorate the suite. And you will find a place that will carve John's likeness in ice, or Corbin will never speak to you again." She strutted her way into the entrance hall and placed her hand on the doorknob. "Do I make myself clear?"

She threw open the door where Corbin stood in the hallway with his hand up in a fist, seemingly ready to knock. How'd all these people appear at my door without a key to the elevator? Corbin's eyes were wide with surprise and mildly amused to see Westward.

"Mr. Lane! We we're just talking about you. Don't leave too big of a mess around here. I wouldn't want to see poor Dottie work too hard."

I casually closed the door behind Westward, not wanting to seem worked up in front of Corbin.

"What was that all about?" Corbin waited for me to close the door.

"Nothing. You know, Westward being Westward." I raced through the suite's entrance hall toward the kitchen, hoping to leave my previous conversation behind. "Do you want a drink?"

"Got it covered." He pulled a bottle of wine out of his coat.

"Did I ever tell you that you rock?" I searched the kitchen for a pair of wine glasses. Corbin didn't drink much, even though he owned a bar, so I knew he was thinking of me when he stopped at the liquor store before coming up to the suite.

"You haven't for quite a few years." He poured the red wine into the glasses. Corbin had changed from the twelve-year-old boy I met by the pond, and even from high school graduation. His athlete's body had matured. Here in the suite, his muscles were evident through the dark blue shirt that fit snugly around his chest. After venturing through a few awkward phases, his hair was now styled in a sultry way that made his blue eyes smolder. But maybe that was just the look he reserved for me. His eyes had that look as he handed me my glass of wine.

"No, I haven't." I paused, not sure if I was ready to go there. "You know why." I carried my glass to the sofa and placed it on the end table, folding my legs beneath me as I sat. Corbin settled in beside me. I leaned my head against his shoulder.

His fingers stroked my hair along the temple, and the feeling brought me back to high school. To the first time he kissed me by our pond, two lovesick teenagers ready to take their five-year friendship to the next level.

"You know …" His voice was a whisper. "It hurt me as much as it hurt you. I lost you that day. But what hurt me the most was that you didn't trust me."

His fingers paused. We sat in silence, both of us probably anxious to have a conversation that was seven years overdue.

I stared at my wine glass. "What if you saw some guy kissing me? How'd you feel if the person you cared about more than anything in the world cheated on you?"

Corbin lifted his shoulder away from my cheek, gazing into my eyes. His fingers trembled as he took my hand. "I'd be crushed, but I'd still come to you. I'd still wait to see what you had to say."

I continued to look into his eyes, unwavering in my determination to finish this discussion. "I died that day. I mean, in college I went through the motions of dating, but no one ever changed how I felt about you." I glanced away for a moment, willing my tears to stay put in my eyes. "How could anyone come close?"

His hand had moved to my shoulder as I spoke, his fingers drifting along the silk of my bathrobe. He cupped my face with his free hand. By this point I had to choke down the tears. How could I do this to him? To Shay? I tried to focus on the original plan that was miles away from Quandary.

Corbin's eyes searched mine while he leaned me back against the sofa cushion, his body pressed lightly to me. "I love you. And now that you know the truth, I'm not afraid to tell you that. I've loved you since I was twelve years old. I love that you don't take anything from anybody. I love that you bite your lower lip when you're trying to rein in that attitude." He brushed my lower lip with his finger while I laid there, shell-shocked and speechless. Even when we dated, Corbin never spoke those words to me. It was almost as if the three words were taboo. So, to hear them now … after all these years.

"I love that when you come into the bar, every man's eyes are on you, but the only man you look at is me." He blushed slightly at this last statement, but I continued to lay there silent with my heart beating out of my chest. When my mouth still refused to move, Corbin bent down and found my lips with his, gently, trying to coax mine out of their dead state. Surrender came when I let my heart take over for my head. Wrapping my arms around his neck, I pulled him closer, moving my lips with his. The kiss was familiar, like our lazy summer kisses down by the pond, but it also held urgency. Like this was our last chance and we were submerged below the pond's surface, the weight of the water pushing in on me from all sides. The guilt surged through me as I resurfaced from the kiss, gasping for air.

Corbin rested his head against my chest. My erratic heartbeat was that of someone who knew that fairytales were seldom as perfect as the childhood stories made them out to be. Cinderella never had to decide between Prince Charming and her best friend George down the lane.

Corbin lifted his head to look at me again. "Will you go to the dance with me on Saturday?"

I smirked at the high-schoolish tone to the question. "I can't, Corb." I pushed his dark hair out of his face and sighed, thinking about the ruby red dress and slippers that hung in my closet. Thinking about Shay and my plan to escape the traps of my small town.

Corbin sat up. "Are you already going with someone?" He didn't have to say Shay's name for me to know that's who he meant.

"Are you jealous?" I pulled myself up, reaching over to ruffle his hair.

"If he's taking you to the dance, I am." Corbin moved his head away from my hand. "He doesn't know you like I do. He's only known you for three days."

"Maybe not, but he knows I'm an orange." I still wondered if I'd ever get to see Shay's paintings.

"A what?" Corbin almost laughed.

"An orange." I stood up to refill my glass of wine. I needed to relax if we were going to continue down the road of this conversation. "He said that orange is my color because I'm vibrant and full of life, and if he painted me that would be the dominant color in the picture." I placed my filled glass on the side table.

Corbin took my hand and pulled me down onto his lap. I snuggled my face into his chest, the warmth radiating through the cotton of his shirt.

"You are an orange, Dot."

I looked up at him. "And you're a blue."

"Because I make you sad?" He ran his fingers through my hair.

"Not at all." I said turning my head to look up at him. "Blue is the first thing I think of when I see you. Your eyes are the most amazing shade of blue I've ever seen. But it's more than that. Blue's so calm and peaceful, like the ocean. But it's also strong and stable at the same time. Do you know what I mean?"

His chest heaved a big sigh, before he eased my head back down against it. "Whatever you say, dear." We sat there for a moment, soaking up Corbin's calm vibes. "Are you going to answer my question?"

"No, I'm not going to the dance with Shay." I was unsure if I should tell him the truth, but I wanted him to hear it from me. "Westward's throwing some big party for John Mellencamp's birthday in my suite and she's forcing me to decorate and serve at it."

"How can she force you to do that?" Corbin moved out from under me again and stood up to refill his glass.

"Threatened my job." I lied. I took a sip of wine and prayed that my little white lie wouldn't come back to bite me in the butt.

"She forgets who her boss is." Corbin frowned. "Besides, I actually know what she makes. Where's she getting the money to throw a huge party?"

"Don't know, but I'm supposed to find someone to carve Mellencamp's likeness in ice by Saturday. That won't be cheap."

He turned on the stereo in the entertainment center. "Well, let's forget about it tonight." He lit a candle sitting on the kitchen counter before reaching over the sofa to take my hand.

The lights of the city stretched out like a wonderland far below, lighting the suite in a myriad of colors. Corbin held me close as we danced to the slow jazz on our own private dance floor. I won't say there wasn't any kissing involved, but like a gentleman, he left at midnight, so we could rest up for our early morning.

As he leaned down to kiss me goodnight before disappearing behind the elevator doors, I whispered in his ear. "Thank you."

Afterward, lying in my gigantic king-sized bed alone, I wrapped myself in the satin sheets, thinking about love and the color blue.

Chapter 15

My beige pantsuit spoke volumes as I took one last glance in the mirror before heading to my first workshop of the day. I had a wisp of hair on each side held back by a clip, giving me a clean, professional look. The ride down the central elevator to the lobby took mere seconds, as I used all my brainpower to try to will the elevator to come to a screeching halt, broken beyond repair. You can probably guess that it didn't work.

My first workshop was entitled *Discovering the Unique Talents in Each of Your Students*, and I knew Shay was signed up for the same class. I thought about how I failed miserably in my mission to let Corbin down easily last night. I cringed, thinking about the questions Shay might ask.

Tapping my pen against the notebook, I leaned against the back wall and I pictured myself becoming one with the wallpaper. As the presenter readied her materials in the front of the room, she dropped a couple dozen papers all over the floor. I took a breath realizing someone else in the room was as nervous as me. A heavyset man with dark hair and glasses sat down in the two seats next to me. I closed my eyes and thanked Jesus. Lack of proximity meant there was no way Shay could ask me about last night, yet.

He strolled in two minutes before the class was supposed to start, two cups of coffee in his hands. Seeing me hidden in the corner, Shay managed to ask the man next to me to move over a seat. Dang it.

"I missed you last night." He handed me the coffee. The warm cup felt wonderful in a room that was much too cold for those of us lacking extra padding. "Did you get some stuff worked out with Pretty Boy?"

"Welcome to *Discovering the Unique Talents in Each of Your Students*." The presenter shared a thin smile as she kneaded her hands. I thanked God for her timing. So far, He was really on my side today. "My name is Denise Simmons. Please speak up if you have any questions during the next two hours."

About thirty minutes into her far-from-interesting presentation, Shay passed me a piece of paper. I guess note passing wasn't just for second graders anymore.

> *I feel sorry for this woman's students. She just goes on and on. Presenting is definitely not her unique talent. Anyway, tell me about last night.*

I turned the piece of paper over and wondered how much I should tell. My head felt like I just got off one of those rides at the county fair where you spin until you stick to the wall and the floor drops out. I scribbled out a lie and a little bit of the truth on the paper to appease him for a while.

> *Corbin asked me to the dance on Saturday, but I told him no. He's a little sensitive, so I only told him a few things about us.*

He took the note, read it, and began to write again.
> *Do you want to go to the dance with me? It's our last night.*

After reading his words, I closed my eyes and rested my head against the wall again. Shay had no intention of continuing our relationship after Vegas. My intuition read that clearly between the lines. What good did it do being wild and free if you had to do it alone, going from one thing to the next, a drifter in a lonely world of strangers? This gave me the first real glimpse into Shay's life. Nothing solid to hold onto except his job at the school in Amarillo.

When we left the classroom, exhausted from boredom, Shay took my hand. We decided to have lunch at the little cafeteria in the basement of the hotel. The tables were crowded, but we found an empty one near the cash registers.

"Why do all the women working at the cash registers look like my mom with a hairnet and a mustache? I thought the casinos in Vegas only hired hot women. Isn't that some kind of unspoken rule?" Shay sat down in the seat next to me, his eyes dancing in his own humor. It was easy to see why I was attracted to him. I was also attracted to chocolate, but that didn't mean it was good for me.

"How many girls have you dated?" I swirled my straw around in my drink.

Shay, seemingly surprised by my question, ran his fingers through his hair and then took a drink of his soda. "You mean girls with mustaches? Only one. But, honestly, I was drunk and it was dark. Except for those flashing strobe lights—but you know how you can't see anything clearly with them going."

"I'm being serious." I didn't know if he even knew me well enough to pick up on my annoyed state.

"Probably about ten this year. But you know what kind of girls I date. They don't mean anything, just a roll in the sack."

He literally had no fear or shame. We spent hours and hours BS-ing and then having fun at night, but I never asked him about the things that really mattered. I turned into one of his one-night stands. Shay didn't attach strings to his relationships. He was like a kite that broke free from its string, soaring through the sky without a care.

"I don't think this is going to work." I was a lot more positive in my feelings than I had been the night before.

"What's not going to work?" He was so clueless for a brilliant AP physics teacher.

"Us, Shay." I kept my eyes on him, but he looked down at his plate.

"Oh." He stuck his fork into his salad.

"There are a lot of things I like about you. You bring out the best in me, and sometimes I love that you have no inhibitions. I like that you see my wild side and know how to paint a totally different picture of my life that nobody else sees." My cheeks grew hot with embarrassment. "Not to mention you're an incredible lover."

"But." Shay started reaching his hand across the table to find mine. "You're in love with him."

"This is about us, Shay." I absently drew circles on his finger. "At twenty-four, I have to look at my future, and I don't see a future with you. I need a string to hold onto, and you're not the type of person who's held down by strings."

"You know I'm ready to be that person." Shay lowered his voice with the intimacy of the conversation. "I told you the night we were in the Painted Desert. You make me want to be a better man. I've never cared about my wellbeing before, not that I was suicidal, but I thought life was about getting the next high. That's why sometimes it seems like I don't have a brain cell left. But when I met you, I knew life could be different."

"And it still can." I had my mind made up. "Now that you know what you want, go out and get it. Women find you very attractive, and there are others like me out there."

"But you know the saying, 'You always want what you can't have.'" Shay's eyes gleamed as he glanced across the room.

"That's not a reason to be with somebody. You'll always be one of my best friends. We've been through too much together."

Instead of responding, Shay leaned toward me and kissed me on the lips. I let him, as a good-bye to our physical relationship, but pulled back when I heard Corbin's voice.

"Dottie, Shay, I'm sorry to interrupt." Corbin held a sandwich and a drink; his face held disappointment. My mind instantly reliving the dream from my bedroom—but now it was turning into a real-life nightmare.

"Hi there, Pretty Boy, I didn't see you coming." Shay's eyes held onto their mischievous gleam and I understood the meaning behind his kiss. I kicked him under the table.

"Sit down, Corb." I pleaded with him, but his eyes failed to meet mine. This was it. He was feeling the way I felt when I thought he betrayed me in high school.

"I'll look for another seat." Corbin glanced around the tables. "You two were having a private conversation."

I shot a look at Shay. He'd better fix this mess he put me into or I'd never forgive him.

He stood up. "I was just leaving, Pretty Boy." He wrapped Corbin in a manly hug and then pecked him on the cheek. "We're very affectionate in Amarillo." He tipped his cowboy hat at me, and left without another word.

"Now that is a strange man." Corbin pulled up the seat next to me. "First he enjoys dancing with Westward, now this. But for some reason, I don't think that kiss with you was part of his over affectionate roots."

"No." I sighed. "I was telling him good-bye, but I don't think he's going to give up so easily." I looked down. "And there's something I need to tell you. See, Shay and I ..."

" ... Kissed." Corbin nodded. "I know there was a lot of flirting going on between the two of you. He couldn't take his hand off your leg last night at the dinner table. It's not like I own you, I just hoped that maybe you felt the same way now that you knew the truth."

"Corbin, I'm not sure if I can go back to Quandary. I can't live life wilting away in Kansas, and now that Westward's there, life is beyond intolerable."

He reached across the table for my hand. Tina and Zeke came up from the register line.

"Man this place is boring during the day. Bunch of teachers trying to learn. What fun is that?" Tina plopped down in the seat next to Corbin. "Let's go out tonight and throw down some cash."

"I'd like that." I tried to put off preparing for Westward's party. "Maybe we could drive down to Caesar's or something. You in, Corb?"

Corbin stood up. "Sounds like fun, but I've got to meet with Westward tonight to discuss the information we gleaned from the workshops today." He turned to me. "Don't worry, Dot. You don't have to show up. Of course, she'll expect you, but I'll tell her you weren't feeling well."

"You sure?" I hated the way he always took the heat for me. Westward knew this was the way he ticked and was sure to be suspicious.

Corbin bent down and gave me a quick peck on the lips. "Not a problem, dear." He dumped his tray and left through the side doors.

"So it looks like you made your decision." A huge grin stretched across Tina's face. She looked like she just rolled out of bed, a bowl of cereal on her tray. Zeke wore his conference nametag over his breast pocket and had already devoured half a sandwich.

I decided to play along with her game. "You should've seen the good-bye kiss Shay gave me." If I was heartless like Tina, I would have strung both guys along until they both hated me—but I couldn't do that any longer.

"Oooh, do tell!" Tina bent her body forward like we were teenagers spreading a juicy piece of gossip. I gave her a love smack on the forehead, pushing her back into her seat.

"I don't kiss and tell." I pulled out my schedule to see where my next class was located. It started at one, so I had about an hour to call around town and see if someone was willing to carve a man in a hunk of ice for me.

"Ok, then, here's the real question." Tina kept going. "Who are you going to the dance with?"

"No one." I continued looking at my schedule.

Maybe Tina needed a dose of her own medicine. "Who are you going to the dance with?" Zeke stopped chewing for a moment, probably to listen to her answer.

"I'm keeping my options open," Tina said. "Maybe I'll go stag and find my prince charming while I'm there. Of course, they're all teachers, so where's the money in that?" Zeke turned back to his sandwich—I think his hopes were further diminished.

"Well, I'm sure some great guy will ask you before Saturday." I gave Zeke a wink when Tina wasn't looking. Matchmaker wasn't a hat I usually wore, but when it was painfully obvious that Zeke wanted to ask her, I had to do something to boost his courage.

~~~

The phone directory listed at least fifty party-planning businesses in Las Vegas, so I started with the first one listed which happened to be Adam's Animal House. From my disjointed conversation with Adam, I found out that he mainly hosted parties with strippers. Tempting as it was to really liven up Westward's party, I moved down to the next place: Clowns, Cakes, and Celebrations. The name held a little more promise, so I dialed the number. The woman who answered gave me the name of a local artist who specialized in ice sculptures, so I called him and arranged a meeting for that afternoon.

My next class provided entertainment and a break from Shay and Corbin. The presenter was a hoot and really knew her stuff. She made me think about my own second graders in a whole new light. I was certain my newly acquired knowledge would benefit our entire school. The class ended at three, so I quickly changed for my meeting with Barry, the ice sculptor, at his studio twenty minutes across town.

My Jeep sat in the parking garage where I left it on Tuesday, and the warm air outside put me in a good mood, so I skipped to my driver's side door. Inserting the key, the engine refused to turn over. I tried again, but for some reason—probably that it was older than God—the Jeep wouldn't start. I pulled out my cell phone.

"Hi, Barry, it's me, Dottie." I turned the key again. Nothing. "My car won't start, so I thought with the time crunch, I won't bother looking at your work. Just consider yourself hired. You'll find a picture of him on the internet." I hung up, stepped out of the car, and stomped back to the door to the lobby. Frustration had obliterated any spring in my step.

Chapter 16

The late afternoon sunlight blasted through the windows of the suite as I slipped out of my clothes and into a robe. I started for the shower, then hesitated, before hoisting my suitcase onto the bed. Unzipping the front pocket, I took a copy of my resume and set it on the table by the window. Two years of experience at a tiny nothing school, a bachelor's degree from the University of Kansas, high school head cheerleader—all which were hardly anything to write home about. If I could work for a big school district like the one in Las Vegas, my career might take off.

After a long shower, I dressed in my khaki skirt and white-off-shoulder blouse, ready for a night on the town. The phone next to my bed rang as I put on my gold hoop earrings.

"Fantasy Suite." I was expecting Tina.

"Our debriefing starts in ten minutes," Westward barked. "So don't be late!"

I flopped back onto the bed after hanging up the phone, took a deep breath and released it out slowly. To let this woman know how I really felt about her, that I detested her with every cell in my body, now that would be a true fantasy. And when I secured a job in Vegas, I was going to do it. I'd let Maxine Westward know that if I had to choose between saving her from certain death or saving a terrorist, I would choose the terrorist every

… single … time. Because the day she stepped into Quandary Elementary, she terrorized our little town and caused the greatest upheaval since Stu Hankins, a known sex offender, became the school bus driver.

Resigned to my captive plight, I rolled back over and phoned Tina to let her know that our night of frivolous gambling was out the window.

Westward opened the door to her room with her usual sneer. A gush of ghastly perfume that rushed out into the hallway caused me to hold my breath. Her curtains were drawn and the air was still giving the room a stifling feel. A few papers were laid out across one of the beds.

"A little underdressed for a business meeting, Dottie." Westward gathered the papers on the bed and placed them in a neat stack on the table by the window.

Sitting down, I crossed my legs, not giving a care about Westward's opinion on my outfit. "Should've worn the fancy red number I have up in my closet, since I won't be wearing it to the dance."

Westward moved about the room, picking up the various items. She failed to look at me. "Do you know if Shay has a date to the dance?"

I imagined Westward as many things, a witch currently topped that list, but a cougar? A cougar! Although my face still held the same expression, my insides were splitting open so it took me a minute or two to compose myself. "Um, I don't really know what Shay is doing for the dance, Maxine. Besides that, I thought you had a party to host."

She now stood still in front of the mirror, running a comb through her spiky red hair. "I thought the two of you shared everything, since you shacked up together."

"No." I refused to let her get to me. "He asked me, but I told him I had to serve at your stupid little party. But since you plan to end it early, maybe I can go to the dance."

"Oh, Dottie." Maxine turned toward me. "I'm sorry to have given you the wrong impression. You'll be cleaning up your suite well into the night so we can leave early on Sunday. Need to be back to work on Monday."

There was a knock on the door.

"Whatever, Maxine." I stood up to answer it. "I'm not sure how I'm getting back anyway because my car's not starting."

"Too bad for you." Maxine sat down in the chair at the desk as Corbin came in.

"What's too bad?" Corbin set his messenger bag down on the bed.

"Dottie just told me I'll have to dock her pay because she won't be back for work on Monday." Westward didn't look up from the paper she was writing on, but her pen paused waiting for Corbin's response.

"Maxine." Corbin sighed. "You can't dock her pay when she's on a business trip."

"Mr. Lane, I'm afraid I'm going to have to let the rest of the board know about how protective you've become of Ms. Gale on this trip. It is very unprofessional, and an inappropriate relationship with an employee is just cause to have you impeached from the board."

"What the hell are you talking about?" I refused to guard my words. "Corbin and I have been friends for a long time. The board knows this, the whole town knows this. You think you can just fly into Quandary and change everything? Well, you're going to have to get rid of both of us first, and that won't go over well with most people."

Maxine's pen continued to scrawl some type of list on the paper in front of her. I hated that woman more than anyone I ever hated in my life. I went into the bathroom to calm my passive aggressive tendencies that just morphed into overtly aggressive feelings ready for action.

The standard bathroom in her room was a lot smaller than the grand one in my suite, and theme-based, with a green shower curtain and royal throne toilet. I snooped around the cabinets, pulling something I thought was a curling iron out of a bag, but quickly dropped it back in when I realized it was a personal massager.

Maxine pounded on the locked door. "Get out here, Dottie. We're ready to start."

Yeah, yeah, I thought, scrubbing my hands. I'd be out there on my own time. "Can't a girl use the bathroom?"

Another toiletry bag hung from a towel hook. I stood with my hand frozen in the air, reflecting on the unsettling results of my last inquiry into Maxine's personal life. Unzipping the top, I found some hairspray, a large amount of make-up, and facial cleanser. Maxine pounded on the door again as I zipped up the bag. A small swatch of material got stuck about halfway across the top, so I yanked it to pull it free like I had done numerous times for my students on their coats. Instead of releasing the material from the zipper, the cloth pulled away from the outside of the bag, revealing an inside compartment.

My heart pounded as the banging on the door grew more insistent. I reached down the hole and pulled out a large wad of money. The top bill was a hundred. I fanned the money in my hand, realizing that every single bill was a Franklin. I placed the money on the floor and pulled out several pieces of paper. Unfolding the envelope sized notes I saw three checks made out to Maxine from Quandary Elementary for five thousand dollars each. Percy Jones's signature scrawled the approval.

"Do I need to break down this door, Dottie?" Westward was screeching as I closed up the bag the best I could. I opened the door feeling numb and miles away. As much as I said that I wanted to get away from Quandary, I didn't want some stranger coming into town taking advantage of the children.

I walked like a zombie out of the bathroom, and into the bedroom. Westward's face was beet red and pearls of sweat dripped from her brow.

"Maxine wanted to go over some of the plans she had to improve the school." Corbin sat in a chair by the desk with his right leg crossed over his left. He was so innocent, oblivious to the crime being played out right under his nose.

Westward eyed me, but I was able to shake off my zombie-state, and I played the game well. "Let's hear it, Maxine."

She sat down in her chair again, picking up the pieces of paper, but my eyes glazed over. Physically in the room but mentally miles away, I wanted to go back into the bathroom and take the school's money, calling her out in front of Corbin. But I also knew she still held Shay over my head and she wouldn't hesitate to use that card.

Westward blabbed on about playing classical music in the hallways throughout the day. The attentive Dottie would have told her that it was absurd and would drive most of the teachers to a mental institution. But I kept quiet. She mentioned something about changing the color palettes of the classrooms after some new-aged freak recommended it in one of her workshops today. I just grunted in agreement.

When Westward finally took a break and went to the bathroom, Corbin sat down on the bed next to me. "Snap out of it, Dottie." He brushed his hand across my forehead, his blue eyes on mine. "Are you alright?"

"Just tired." I was more than ready to crawl into bed and forget this night ever happened.

From the look in Corbin's eyes, I knew that he understood that something was wrong. How could I hide it from him? Corbin knew I would have snapped at Westward's ideas, ready to fight her to the end, even if I was running on fumes. He also knew how to tell when I was miles away, thinking about something so devastating it had an impact on everything I held close. My sophomore year in high school, I came home to the news that my wayward father had died. I never knew him, but now I would never have the chance. I became a zombie for an entire week that time, someone I didn't know or care to know. Corbin helped me through that time, and knew the warning signs better than anyone.

The bathroom door opened. "We're leaving, Maxine." Corbin's voice left little room to argue. "We'll join you in the morning for a breakfast meeting at the café on the first floor." He didn't wait for a response, but took my hand and led me to the door.

Corbin didn't talk, or force me to talk, all the way up to my suite. I didn't object to his gentle prodding down the hallway and into the elevator. I woke up enough to find the key in my purse so he could insert it into the slot in the elevator, pushing the buttons to take us to my floor. Still, Corbin didn't speak as he opened the door to the suite. He turned the dimmer light on low before leading me to the bedroom. I sat down on the bed, kicking off my shoes while he turned down my covers. The pillow provided the comfort I needed to erase—well not quite erase, but to dim, like the lights in the hallway—the shock of the secret I held.

Corbin kneeled down beside the bed, taking hold of my hand. "I know something happened back there, but don't worry about it now. Just sleep." He leaned forward, kissed my forehead, and left the room.

My sleep was restless, full of nightmares produced by my overactive subconscious. I had hall duty as the students came in after being dropped off by their buses. A blizzard whipped snow across the barren Kansas land outside the school, so the children rushed inside to the warmth and security of the building. Westward stood in the vestibule, stopping each child as they entered. The students were handing her something, and those who refused were pushed outside into the freezing temperatures, locking the door behind them. Concerned, I made my way toward the witch as she cackled with glee ready to shove a first grader outside.

"What are you doing, Ms. Westward?" I grabbed the young child and held him to me.

"Collecting lunch money." She rifled through another child's backpack. "Another naughty child bringing in cold lunch!" She tossed the Barbie lunch box into a pile of assorted boxes and paper bags before opening the door for another victim. I stared in horror at the huddle of children outside in the parking lot.

Some had early signs of frostbite, while others were frozen solid into a block of ice.

"You witch!" I screamed. "Stealing money from children, and throwing them out into the cold if they have nothing." Opening a nearby fire extinguisher box, I pulled out the clip on the device, pushed down the handle, and covered Westward with foam. She physically started to shrink in front of me as if her legs were descending through a trapdoor in the linoleum.

"What have you done? I'm melting. You can't do this to me! You're nothing but a worthless tramp." Only the top part of her body appeared to be above the floor now as her legs shriveled into oblivion. But her mouth remained above the floor, so she continued to screech. "I'm melting! I'm melting! Oh, what a world! Who would have thought a little brat like you could destroy my beautiful wickedness!"

In moments, Westward's body was gone, including her mouth, thank God. All that was left was the pile of her hideous clothes and some dry ice smoke for effects. I scrambled to the door to let the students in. Mike had to get the dolly to wheel in the frozen ones, taking them to defrost in the kitchen.

My suite was pitch black when I opened my eyes, the Westward extortion dream still freshly buzzing through my brain. When I turned on the light, a glass of water sat on my nightstand. I was extremely thirsty, but reaching for the glass, I knocked the phone to the floor. Corbin came into the room as I lifted the it back to its rightful place.

"You stayed." I pulled the covers back around me even though I was still dressed.

"You worried me." He sat down on the end of the bed. "You left me last night, like that time with your dad." He moved closer, putting his hand on top of the blankets. "Are you alright?"

"I'll be fine." I took a sip of water. "Some Westward junk that I need to work out on my own." Everything within me wanted to tell Corbin about Westward stealing money from the school, but I wasn't ready for him to know the truth about Shay. Even in my dream, the pained image of his face was too much when he learned the truth. It would definitely be too much to take if it became a reality.

Corbin gazed into my eyes for a long time, probably trying to draw the truth out of them, but gave up, knowing I could be as stubborn as a mule. "Why don't you get dressed and we can get a cup of coffee before meeting with Westward?"

The morning blurred by as I sat with the woman whose secret I kept—and who held onto mine. Corbin appeared oblivious to our constant mind games, but I knew he picked up on some of them.

"Dottie, why don't you hire a DJ for the party instead of a live band." Westward changed the subject from our discussion on offering foreign language at the school.

"Oh, come on, Maxine. I'm sure you can afford a live band. You have much more cash than a teacher." Westward glared across the table at me, daring me to cross the line.

She uncrossed her legs and then crossed them again, probably contemplating her next attack.

Corbin shifted in his seat, apparently more uncomfortable with our nonverbal attacks than our verbal ones. "So, I think we should approach the rest of the board with our idea of a French class after school on Tuesdays and Thursdays."

"Excuse me, Mr. Lane." Westward held up a hand to him in a gesture to stop. "I want to tell Miss Gale one more essential detail about my party before we continue with other business."

"By all means." I could tell that Corbin was slightly put out that Westward treated him like an annoying little child.

Payback time. I hinted to her sin, now she was going to hint to mine. I almost scooped up my notebook and left for my first class, but I'm not one to run away from a fight.

"Last night you mentioned a red dress. Make sure you wear it to the party. I invited Shay Fields, and I'm sure he, as well as some of my other guests, will be pleased."

"Maybe I'll just loan it to you. After all, you're the one trying to please him." This time I did stand up to go, leaving my two co-workers silent in my wake.

Chapter 17

My morning class was held in half of the grand ballroom, the large space separated by an accordion partition. The presenter, an elementary principal from someplace in California, was actually pretty good. I gained an odd sense of comfort from being surrounded by people who knew absolutely nothing about Dottie Gale from Kansas. Instead of trying to meet someone for lunch, I grabbed a quick bite and went to the atrium.

Hundreds of tables surrounded the room. Teachers milled around here and there like ants; none of them seemed to have any real purpose. Small charter schools in Kansas didn't have the funds to purchase a new curriculum, so I avoided the publishers, but instead found the Las Vegas school district representatives. Seven men and women dressed in interview attire sat along the long table, reviewing resumes with potential employees. Standing in line behind a thin, older woman, I took my resume folder and tapped it against my leg. I shifted my weight from foot to foot, telling myself that the nerves came from having to interview, but I knew that wasn't the truth. Even though my relationship with Corbin held a new light that it hadn't seen in years, my promise to myself was to at least go through with the interview, and I don't break my promises.

A young man with a bowtie and a nametag that said Reed Tollemache shook my hand a little too enthusiastically as I sat down in the metal chair across from him. Placing his reading glasses on the bridge of his nose, he ran through my resume, stopping a few times to ask me questions.

"Well, Ms. Gale, you are a fresh, young talent. Exactly what the Las Vegas school district is looking for."

"Thank you, Mr. Tollemache." I was unsure how to handle the glowing compliment.

"We'd need to speak to your current principal, and I know it's October, but I have a teacher taking off for maternity leave in a couple of weeks. She plans on missing the remainder of the school year, and I think you'd fit right in with our staff." Reed beamed at me like I was the greatest find since the Hope Diamond.

"Wow, that's so soon." I placed my resume back into my bag, not sure if I was ready to up and leave Quandary … to leave Corbin. "I thought there wouldn't be anything open until next school year. I'd have to sell my house."

"No worries there, Ms. Gale. We have a temporary housing allowance for new teachers exactly in your position. It'd give you time to sell your house without having to pay the rent."

"This is all so sudden." I stood up, but kept my hand on the chair to settle myself. "Can I get back to you?"

"Of course." He reached down and handed me a business card from the tray on his table. "My personal cell phone number is on there, and I'll be around through Sunday afternoon. Don't hesitate to call."

"I won't, Mr. Tollemache. Thank you for the generous offer." It was a generous offer, but I didn't expect it.

"Please call me Reed." He reached out his hand and held onto to mine a little longer than I deemed comfortable for a professional situation. Then he sat back down ready for his next interview.

I took the afternoon off to prepare for Westward's party. Using the concierge, I found a party store within walking distance. I paid for the entire purchase myself, not wanting to end up in prison for spending school funds that Westward gave me. My only concern was the ice sculpture, which I knew was going to cost way more than my measly budget could manage. I arranged to pick up the balloons the next day.

When night finally fell on the sleepless city, I was amazed that I managed to avoid both Shay and Corbin the entire day. I spoke to Tina earlier and planned to meet her and Zeke for a night of frivolous gambling. I pulled on my pink dress, wore my hair down, and was out the door at promptly seven o'clock. I know there's no fashion in being prompt, but I was bored.

Tina and Zeke weren't in the lobby, so I checked the casino floor. When I couldn't find them, I sat down at a poker table, ready to play the odds. I'd never gambled before, but Uncle Embry taught me to play poker when his friends came over on Friday nights. They'd let me sit and watch and I learned a lot. I could read every guy's face. When I turned eighteen and they finally let me join in, I should've held back. I did so well they never let me play again.

The dealer handed me my chips and then dealt the cards. I took that time to evaluate the three other players at the table. One was a little old granny, must've been eighty-five years old, but man did she look mean. Her expression didn't change one iota when she set up her cards. The man to my left wore a leather jacket, a ball cap, and heavy gold chains around his neck. A cigar hung from his lips and some cheap brunette hung from his arm. He winked at me when he caught me looking, so I moved on to the last player. She an Asian woman probably in her mid-forties, and I knew in an instant that she was the true player at the table.

After losing several hands, my luck changed and I won with a flush.

"Beginner's luck." Eminem snorted as I raked in the pot. His comment sparked something in me, and I was going to show him that I was the one to beat at this misfit table.

I glanced at his cigar. "Got an extra one of those things?" I loved ticking off his arm ornament. He handed me a cigar and a light, and I puffed the smoke in his face. "Stick around and you'll see who you're dealing with."

I split the next four hands evenly with the Asian woman, who turned out to be every bit of the poker player I thought she might be.

The fifth hand came down to the two of us. My hand contained a ten, three, jack, king, and an ace. All I needed in the flop was a queen. The dealer laid down the flop—the queen of hearts. I chanced a sideways glance at my foe, but her face remained like stone. I knew I had her and my heart began to race. Uncle Embry taught me to play it cool, not reveal too much with my upping of the ante.

She finally folded and I squealed, unable to contain my excitement. Four hundred bucks! Just so you know, that happens to be a lot of money for a teacher who needs to buy an ice sculpture.

Spotting Tina and Zeke at a pair of slot machines across the room, I bowed out gracefully and a lot richer than when I started.

"Hey, girlie." Tina jumped up to give me a hug. "Where've you been?"

"Only winning mucho bucks at the poker table." I held up my tray of chips.

Tina's eyes grew wide. "Where are you taking us?"

"Not going to happen, girlfriend." I spun the chips away from Tina. "This money's already spent on a hunk of ice."

"Well that sucks." Tina frowned. "I thought maybe we could have a girl's night at the Thunder Down Under." She thrust her hips and Zeke looked away. "Speaking of the Thunder Down Under."

I looked up and Shay was moving our way from the blackjack tables, his own tray of chips in hand. He came over to us and put his arm around my waist, whispering in my ear. "Too bad there aren't any firemen in the house, because you're smokin.'"

"Too bad you have the lamest pick-up lines I've ever heard." I laughed. "There's a couple of girls checking you out from the bar. Maybe you could use a few of your lines on them."

Shay glanced in their direction, but shook his head. "I made my New Year's resolution today in the pit of my loneliness."

"But it's October." Tina threw a few quarters into the machine next to her.

"I know." Shay took off his hat. "But it's never too early. I'm going to be a one-woman man. That's if she'll have me." I felt the heat rush to my face with Shay's public proclamation. It was different from before, and I wasn't sure why. Maybe because it was sincere.

I did the only thing I could think of at the moment. I changed the subject and brushed Shay's words aside. "We've got a problem."

The other three looked at me, wondering how we could have a problem at eight o'clock at night in Las Vegas. "My Jeep's dead. I'm not sure how we're going to get home."

"I knew I should've listened to my mother and driven myself here." Zeke hit himself on the forehead. "Why do I always have to go against what she says."

"Are you sure it can't be fixed?" Shay scratched the back of his neck. "We could pool our money together."

"I'm pretty sure." I shifted the tray of chips to my other hand. "My mechanic back in Quandary said the next time it broke down it probably wouldn't be worth fixing."

Out of the corner of my eye, I saw Mr. Oswald walking toward a door next to the cashier's booth. He disappeared inside while a burly-looking man with a handlebar mustache sat on a stool outside the door.

Let me know if there's anything you need.

I knew he was only being polite, but it was worth a try.

"I'll be right back." I crossed the casino floor towards the bodyguard. Shay, Tina, and Zeke followed, unaware of my plan.

The big man wore all black, including a ball cap that almost covered his eyes. His chin jutted out in an unnatural manner below the curls at the tips of his mustache.

"We need to talk to Mr. Oswald." I refused to be afraid of Mr. Beefcake.

"He's not wanting to talk to you." The man did not elaborate any further.

"But I'm Dottie Gale from Kansas." I was confident that the name would permit me immediate passage. "Mr. Oswald said to come see him if I needed him."

"Listen, little lady, I don't care if you're the First Lady of the United States, you're not getting past this door." He folded his arms across his chest and stood in front of the door like an egotistic prison guard.

Turning back to my friends, I shrugged my shoulders in defeat before the door opened from the inside. Mr. Oswald stood there with his car salesman smile, at least a head taller than Mr. Beefcake.

"Tony, Tony." Oswald scolded without taking his eyes off me. "This is the Miss Gale from Kansas that I told you about yesterday. She's to be treated like family while she's here. Come on in, Dottie."

"Can we all come in?" I glanced at my friends. "We have something we have to ask you."

"Of course!" Oswald opened the door wider to let in Shay, Tina, and Zeke. We followed Oswald through a stark white hallway, down a flight of stairs, and through a door that read *private*. Oswald's office reminded me of my suite upstairs in size, but that's where the similarities ended. An enormous desk sat in front of the floor to ceiling windows. A plush green area rug covered the floor where two white leather sofas sat. The rest of the room was completely decorated in black and white. Oswald directed us to have a seat while he rounded his bar and began to pour each of us a glass of wine.

"Nice place you got here, Oz." Tina leaned back on the couch and took in the room. She picked up a magazine from the end table. "Never knew you could do so much with black and white."

Shay helped Oswald carry the glasses from the counter, taking a sip of his along the way. Oswald settled into an oversized armchair next to me, smiling at Tina. "Samuel is an amazing designer. We've really come to understand each other."

"What type of security system do you have in this place?" Zeke scanned the ceiling and walls. "With all those people above us, you must worry about your valuables." He positioned himself next to Tina, but kept an arm's length away to avoid any accidental body contact.

"Mr. Lyons, I find that life is too short to worry all the time. If someone steals something, it can be replaced." Oswald raised an eyebrow and grinned widely at Zeke.

Zeke's jaw dropped. "How-how'd you know …"

"Your name?" Oswald asked. "There isn't a lot that gets by me in my own hotel. You're a guest, aren't you?"

"Yes, but there must be a thousand rooms in the Emerald City."

"Zeke, it doesn't matter how I know your name. It doesn't matter if the stuff in our life gets stolen or broken or lost. What matters are the people in our lives. That we have the courage to tell them how we really feel. Have you done that, Mr. Lyons?"

"I'm …" Zeke tugged at his shirtsleeve. "I'm, uh … not exactly sure what you're talking about." He didn't continue any further.

"And the same goes for you, Miss Steele."

Tina's head shot up from the magazine she browsed through.

"You've got to tell people how you feel and stop treating them like your personal doormats."

"Hey, Ozzy, now you're getting a little personal. What do you know about my heart anyway? You're a high and mighty casino owner who steals money from people every day. You're just full of crap." Tina tossed the magazine back on the table and went to the other room.

Oswald didn't follow her, but Zeke did.

"Is it time for my lecture?" Shay finished off his glass of wine. He refilled each glass on the table.

"Do you need a lecture, Mr. Fields?" Oswald raised his eyebrows.

"Don't tell me you're some kind of sinister psychologist that influences others through his money and power, because that's really not what I need right now." Shay downed his glass in one swig. "My father thought he could use his oil money to get me to go to some fancy Ivy League school. Said he needed a good lawyer for his company. He just wanted me to appear successful in front of the people he ran with. An artistic high school teacher does not equal success in his book."

"So you rebelled?" Oswald played the intruding psychologist role well. It surprised me that Shay was opening up to him.

"Hell, yeah. Got into everything I could that would tick him off. But I think my rebellious phase is about over. I've discovered a lot of things about myself the past couple of days." Shay looked at me. "Like I don't need to please my father, but I don't need to antagonize him anymore, either. I might even give up the hotrod racing with the kids on Tuesday nights."

"Sounds like someone who is using his brain to drive his choices instead of his emotions. The former will definitely take you further." Oswald glanced over to the bedroom where Zeke and Tina came out, hand in hand. The old guy's drivel must have had some kind of effect on them.

"Guess who's got a date for the dance tomorrow?" Tina threw her arms around Zeke's neck and kissed him on the lips.

"How many guesses do we get?" Shay rolled his eyes at me. "I know it's not Dottie. At least that's what she tells me."

Ignoring Shay, I turned to Oswald to find his eyes already fixed on me.

"Now what can I do for you, Dottie?"

"I really hate to bother you with this, Mr. Oswald. If I didn't feel responsible for my friends here, I probably would have found another way." I couldn't even look the man in the eyes. Maybe Spiderman discovered that with great power comes great responsibility, but that didn't mean that a rich man couldn't be a tightwad.

"What do you need?" Oswald leaned his body forward in his chair, urging me to continue.

"My car is as good as dead and I'm supposed to drive Shay and Zeke home on Sunday." The words were out and I knew the worst he could tell me was no.

"You, young lady, happen to be in luck." Oswald stood up to look out the window. The fountains of the casino across the street danced to the music. "I have a business meeting in Oklahoma City on Sunday afternoon and I plan to take my private jet. Flagstaff and Amarillo have small airstrips where I could drop off Zeke and Shay." He glanced at Tina, raising an eyebrow. "And maybe another passenger, if necessary." His eyes returned their penetrating gaze to me. "Would you happen to have a friend who could pick you up in Oklahoma City?"

"That'd be amazing, Mr. Oswald." I gushed, unable to control my excitement.

"Good." Oswald placed his empty glass on the table. "Then it is all arranged. Now, if you will excuse me, we all have a busy day tomorrow and I know I need some shut-eye."

"Not a problem." I stood up with my three friends. "Thank you again."

"Mr. Fields." Oswald opened the front door for us. "Could you stay behind for a few minutes? There's something I'd like to discuss with you."

"As long as it doesn't have to do with my Freudian feelings for my father." Shay stopped beside the door. "I'll see you in a little while, Dottie."

Tina and Zeke were giddy in their newfound affection. They left for Zeke's room while I walked to my suite alone, satisfied with my accomplishments for the night. I had money to pay for the stupid ice sculpture and a way to get back home, which I now knew was where I wanted to be. All that was left was to find a way to get rid of Westward.

Chapter 18

The minute the elevator doors closed, I removed my heels and slid down to the floor, content in my moment of peace. A single red rose with an envelope attached lay on the ground outside the door. I picked it up and smelled it before finding my room key and entering the suite. I slipped it into a glass of water and placed the envelope on my pillow, disappearing into the bathroom for a much-needed shower. Las Vegas teemed with people on the streets below, each with their own life, their own goals, their own dreams. But I knew that my life was in the envelope on my pillow, waiting to be opened, waiting to begin.

～～～

Corbin's mother was the first person that stayed longer than six months in the rental house. Even though I told Corbin I was only friends with him because he successfully netted Old Bill, the truth was I liked him. We found out we had a lot in common as we spent the warm days together down by the pond. He and his mother moved to Quandary when his parents divorced, and she stayed in the rental because it was all she could afford. I told him about my wayward father and the image I had of him on his Harley.

I didn't see Corbin much at school because he was two years older than me. My first day at Quandary High almost killed me for two reasons. First, I still dressed like I was ten, and most of the upperclassman girls appeared to be in their mid-twenties. Second, these girls paid a lot of attention to Corbin, my best friend. That part of his life didn't come with him to the pond or to my house on the snowbound days off from school. It was then that I decided if he was going to be interested in girls in *that* way, then I wanted him interested in me.

Wanda Jo let me borrow some of her clothes, cut the dead-ends off my hair so I could wear it down, and applied make-up to my face. Looking at the new me in the mirror, there was no turning back.

Corbin always saved a seat for me in the lunchroom where we sat among the mature and well-endowed. My hands shook walking up to our usual table as I wondered if I'd still look like a minnow next to the sharks. Would Corbin even notice the difference? I set my backpack on the seat next to him waiting for him to turn.

"Hey, Dot. Could you pick up an extra milk when you go through the line?" He kept his eyes on Michelle, one of the sharks.

"Sure." I tried to keep the disappointment out of my voice. A couple of the girls whispered something to each other and giggled.

"Looks like your girlfriend's trying to impress you." Michelle's voice was both sultry and degrading.

Corbin turned and I darted for the bathroom, sure that the mascara was smeared across my face from the tears. The stalls were empty, so I grabbed the one on the end and blotted my face with toilet paper. The door to the bathroom opened.

"Dottie, come out of there." Corbin's footsteps stopped outside of my stall.

"Get out of here, Corb," I sniffled. "It's the girl's room."

"Only if you're coming with me." He jiggled the handle. "Open the door."

"You'll laugh." But I unlatched the door.

Corbin took a moment to survey the damage, but then stepped forward to hug me. "You look great. Don't listen to those girls, they're idiots." It was at that moment that I fell in love.

~~~

I picked up the envelope and turned it over and over in my hands before finally slipping my fingernail under the seam. I know it seems cliché and girlish, but the letter smelled of him and I held it to my nose, the way I had done with the flower. Then I devoured his words like I did a good book, reading them over and over.

Dottie,

> *I know I haven't been the friend I should've been for you over the past few years. I always knew you deserved more than I could give you. But now that my business is doing well, and after the encouragement you gave me the other night, I feel more confident that I can be there for you.*

> *You drive me crazy. When I see you with another man, I just want to take you into my arms and bring you back to Quandary with me. I know you want to see the world—it's*

*something that's in you. I'll do that for you,
even though I'd be content staying in Kansas,
because anything I've ever wanted is there. But
I'd go to the bush in Africa if you asked me to.*

*I know it's your decision, and I'd be foolish to
believe that I could force you to do anything.
But know that I'm here—I always have been
and I always will be.*

*Love,
Corbin*

Inserting the letter into the envelope, I placed it on the nightstand and let out the breath I'd been holding for the past seven years. Corbin Lane loved me. Not because I had it together, not because I looked sexy in a skintight dress, and not because I was a wild, unpredictable orange. He would love me if all those things disappeared tomorrow. And I knew, even though it would tear him to pieces, that he would still love me if he knew about Shay.

I picked up the phone to call his room, to let him know how much I missed him all day, but a knock on the door interrupted my dialing. My heart picked up its pace, hoping to see Corbin at the door.

I'd never seen Shay's smile so huge. He stood in the hallway with his hands in the pockets of his jeans. He bounced on the balls of his feet like a child who couldn't wait to show his mother his report card.

"Can I come in?" He took in my red silk bathrobe. "Or is this not a good time?"

"No, it's fine." I wondered what happened to his usual pick-up line. Whatever he came up for was really preoccupying his mind. I went to the kitchen and took out the remainder of the bottle of wine Corbin and I opened the night before. "Do you want a drink?"

"Yeah, but make it quick. I don't think I can hold onto this much longer." He jumped over the back of the couch onto the cushions below in a very Cruise-like move. "You can hear me, right?"

"I'm listening." I poured the wine into two glasses. "Don't burst from your news on my account. Does this have to do with Oswald?"

"He's asked me to come to Vegas." Shay looked over the back of the couch to assess my reaction, but I just stared back waiting for the punch line. "He's opening a gallery in the casino and he wants me to run it for him and display some of my art. I'd make way more than my teaching salary."

"That's great, Shay!" I handed him his glass of wine and held up mine. "A toast. To new beginnings and amazing friendships." I clinked my glass against his as his face fell. I knew the day of reckoning was here again.

"I didn't think you were serious before." Shay ran his finger along the rim of his wine glass. "You know, about us being over. I mean, shit, Dottie. You are so unbelievable. You'd learn to love me. You could move to Vegas and teach. I know that's what you want. We could get a place together and start over."

I cupped the side of his rough, stubbly face. I looked into his eyes, trying to hold them, but he kept looking away.

"I love him, Shay. I admitted that to myself when I was fifteen, but I've loved him since the first day we met. I hated him so much when I thought he cheated on me that it became part of my reality. How I felt about my town, my job, the people around me all circled back to my hatred for Corbin. Some wounds run so deep that even when I knew the truth it took me a while to accept it."

Shay continued to look away, so I gently forced him to turn his head toward me. "You helped me discover a lot of things about myself. We were both running away from our skeletons. Your dad's going to give you hell over this whole art thing."

"And do you think I care?"

I removed my hand from his cheek and held his hand. "Not at all. That's what drew me to you. You don't care what anyone thinks."

"I care what you think." Shay was not willing to let go. His light brown hair encircled his face, and his mouth held onto its pout. Despite his maturity, he reminded me of a second grader who'd just had his favorite toy confiscated by the teacher, with no affirmation that he'd ever get it back.

"I know." I leaned my head against his chest. "But I can't help what my heart feels."

Shay ran his fingers through my hair, and I knew that the intimacy of the moment should make me uncomfortable, but he'd never make me feel that way.

"Do you have a band-aid?" Shay asked in a somber voice, his usual boyish flirtation missing. "Because I think I've fallen for you and scraped my heart."

～～～

As I rode down the elevator on Saturday morning to the salon, I doubted Shay would show up for what he called an insult to his manhood. The final classes of the workshop were being held that morning, so teachers roamed the lobby, mingling and networking. A retro metal sign hung above the entrance that read *Wash and Brush Up, Co.*, the doorway a pale shade of mint green. Tina sat on a forest green bench with her legs crossed reading some fashion magazine. Her dark curls were pinned on top her head spilling out in a careless way that I knew it took her hours to produce. The red silk blouse she wore plunged between her cleavage leaving little to the imagination. I suddenly felt extremely underdressed in my black sweats, but honestly, who did I have to dress for in the salon?

"Hey, Dottie." Tina looked up from her reading. "Aren't you excited? This is like the best day of my entire life!" Her breasts jiggled from the buoyancy of the green cushioned bench.

"I can't remember a time when I was more excited." I turned on the sarcasm faucet. "The thought of getting all glammed up to serve Westward and a bunch of stuffy principals excites me to no end. Maybe you could dance with Corbin for me, so he knows I'm there in spirit. Or better yet, I'll ask Shay to do it since he doesn't have a date either."

"I'm sorry." Tina kept her gaze on her shoes most likely trying to think of a way to talk herself out of an awkward moment. Zeke walked in on cue, saving her any further humiliation at the hands of the major downer in the sweat suit.

"Hey ladies." Zeke wrote his name down on the ledger and made his way toward us with a newfound swagger. A black Armani suit and tie made him almost as unrecognizable as his confident posture. I had to admit that he was hot.

"You sure you weren't in here earlier today?" I checked out his suit up close. "Because I've got ten dollars that says you were." I unfolded a bill from my secret stash and held it in front of Zeke.

"Pay up, baby." Zeke yanked the ten dollars from my hand. He called over to a man placing foils in an older woman's hair. "You ever seen me in here before?"

"Oh, no, sugar." The man checked out Zeke's new look. "I'd remember you."

I rested my elbows on my knees, ready to be done with this whole ordeal. "That's how my luck's going today. Better not put out any money on the casino floor. Oswald would wipe me clean."

Three hours later, my mood lifted significantly, I exited the salon arm in arm with Zeke and Tina. I shot a sidelong look at Zeke, amazed that they made him glow. The stylist used some type of facial treatment to scrub away his dried up skin. Tina let go of my arm and twirled across the lobby floor in a lavender dress her stylist provided. Her usually frizzy hair was placed in neat ringlets, highlighting her amazing make-up. I didn't want to even peek in a mirror while I was in there, knowing that I would only get my hopes up for something that wasn't going to happen. My stylist, Sara, gave me a silver strapless dress with knee-high, white go-go boots. She beamed when I came out of the dressing room, but I kept a towel draped over the mirror.

Entering the lobby, I instantly felt like the three of us were on a runway. All eyes shifted in our direction. Far from being a professional model, my heart rate increased from the attention. Tina and Zeke strutted across the room with the confidence of a pair of underwear models. They both stopped in front of the largest gathering of people. Tina pivoted, and continued to swing her hips as she made her way to the elevator. Zeke paused, lifted his collar in a cool fashion, and then followed Tina. All eyes then turned to me, confident they were witnessing some type of fashion show.

I lifted my hand, scrunched my eyes, and gave a little wave to the people. Not the kind of wave a royal would give, but the kind of wave I used to give to Uncle Embry when I was five years old through the window of the school bus. "Please go on with your business," I said. "Nothing to see here." I scooted behind some foliage and then into the nearest bathroom to change back into my sweats.

It's amazing how when you finally admit something to yourself, like that you love someone, the feeling is magnified about a thousand times the next time you see him. Corbin was leaning against the opposite wall when I came out of the bathroom. The same smile crossed his face that I'd seen for fourteen years, but it felt new and different, like trying on a favorite dress for the first time after dropping a bunch of weight and realizing it fit perfectly.

He had his fists in the pockets of his jeans and appeared as if he were expecting to be rejected again after he poured his heart out onto the page of the letter yesterday. I didn't want to play games anymore. I didn't want the rest of our lives to wait any longer. I crossed the short distance between us, standing in front of him, but looking at the buttons on his shirt, searching for the perfect classic movie moment. He lifted my chin, so my eyes found his, sending my heart into overdrive.

"Corbin, I …" He placed his finger on my lips, brushing my hair off my shoulder with his other hand. Then his lips touched mine. And if you think seeing him was magnified from before, to finally kiss Corbin without the guilt was hardly appropriate for a public display of affection. I pulled back in a gasp, flushed from the attention of the onlookers and the intimacy of the moment. He took my hand and pulled me to the elevator, the glass elevator. A small crowd gathered down below as he pushed me against the transparent wall, his mouth finding mine again, then my neck, then my collarbone. My heart continued to pound with wanting.

Exiting the elevator, Corbin lifted me up so my arms were around his neck and my legs around his waist. Rounding the corner to the suite, he stopped, putting me back down on the ground. A man held the handle of a dolly with a large metal box on top. Westward frowned beside him.

"I should've known better than to put my party in the hands of a couple of horny teenagers. I was about to call the manager to get him to open up the room. Give me the key, Gale." I rummaged through my purse, unable to come up with a response. Westward opened the room and directed Barry to wheel the dolly to the center of the room.

"Keep the sculpture in the refrigerated box until a half-hour before the party." Barry let the crate off the dolly. "I'll come back the next day to pick up the box."

I took out his payment from my poker winnings and he left. I was now alone with the person I loved most in the world—and the one I hated worst.

Corbin stayed to help us set up for a party that apparently had quite the guest list. Westward babbled on about the superintendent of some district in California, about the president of some schoolbook publishing company, and perhaps Mr. Oswald himself.

Although we couldn't escape to the bedroom, Corbin took every moment he could to set my heart off again. I bent over to pick a streamer off the floor and he ran his hand along my thigh. While Westward rolled the meat for a deli plate, he followed me into the entry way to help me hang decorations. Corbin had me against the wall for a good three minutes before we heard Westward's heels clinking against the tiles, so we quickly pulled apart.

At four-thirty, Westward proclaimed that I looked a wreck and scooted me into my bedroom to get ready for the party. At four forty-three, a few minutes after I stepped out of the shower, the phone rang.

"We're going to get you out of there," Shay whispered.

"Why are you whispering?"

"Don't people usually whisper when they're on a secret rescue mission?"

"A secret rescue mission? You and what witch-killing army, Shay?" The image of a bunch of people carrying shovels and pitchforks, ready to tie Westward to a stake, made me laugh.

"Zeke, Tina, and me, of course." Shay sounded affronted. "Don't you worry your pretty head. We'll get you to the ball, Cinderella."

"And do you plan on being my Prince Charming?" I thought I had made things clear with Shay the night before. What did you do with someone who wouldn't take no for an answer?

"No." He sighed. "You made it clear what you want. I've got a date anyways."

"Who?" I thought about Westward. It almost made me sick to my stomach visualizing any of my friends with her.

"You'll see at the dance. Just do what we say when we crash Westward's little gathering and don't be an orange. Try being a pink for once."

"What's that supposed to mean? Do you think I get all of your artist lingo?"

"It means, be submissive. You know, sugar and spice and everything nice." Shay laughed. "Never mind, it's not in your nature."

"Shay Fields, if you were here right now I'd throw you out my window and watch you plunge the forty-five stories to your death below." I paused. "And then, I ride down the elevator smoking a cigarette, throw my cigarette onto your corpse and squish it out with my four-inch heels."

"I love you, Dottie Gale," Shay said as he hung up the phone.

Chapter 19

When I came out of the bedroom, the first guests were arriving and Corbin was nowhere to be found. I wore my red dress with Wanda's heels—my ruby red slippers. Westward must have had Corbin remove the refrigerated box from the ice sculpture while I was getting ready, because John Mellencamp and his guitar glistened in the middle of the room. I had to admit, the likeness was actually pretty good.

Westward put me to work serving drinks to the guests while she mingled as a perfect host to the unsuspecting victims. I wasn't exactly sure what she was trying to gain with this party yet. Some type of networking endeavor? If I was going to expose the witch for who she really was, I had to do it tonight in front of some of the best in the field.

A tall woman with glasses and her hair pulled back into a professional bun, stopped to take a drink off my tray. "I'm Rosa Nelson, the superintendent of the Las Vegas school district. Ms. Westward just told me that you volunteered to miss the dance and serve at her party."

"Nice to meet you." I put down a tray to shake her hand. "Yes, I'm always willing to serve my school." I twisted my words so I wouldn't have to lie to the woman.

"You must really respect your boss to give of your time so willingly." Rosa glanced at Westward. Some sort of lively conversation was going on between the witch and another guest. "She's applied for a principal's position at one of our larger schools and she seems like the perfect candidate."

No! I screamed in my head, but I wasn't ready to expose her. Not yet anyways. Not until I could talk to Corbin. I had to let him know first. "It would truly change our school if she left." After all, that was the truth.

Corbin returned an hour later. Scanning the room, his eyes stopped when they landed on me. I twirled around with my tray, showing off the red dress. He shook his head, his beautiful grin crossing his face.

I watched him as he casually crossed the room, stopping to talk to a man in a blue suit, then a woman in a cardigan and a pearl necklace. Westward sat on a stool at the breakfast bar. Making sure his eyes trailed, I went to speak with her.

"I'm going to take a fifteen-minute break. It looks like everyone has a drink. When I get back, I'll start putting the food out."

"Oh, Dottie." Westward had a large man in a tan suit as an audience. "This is Mr. Cucharus. He's the superintendent of the Los Angeles school district."

"Nice to meet you." I shook his hand.

"Dottie's one of my top-notch teachers in Quandary." She looked at me. Something in her eyes told me not to cross her. "I'm sure she'd have plenty to say about the wonderful things that are happening at our school."

"Of course. I just need to take a bathroom break and I'll be back." I slipped away before Westward could stop me, giving Corbin a raised eyebrow before going into my bedroom. I knew he expected something else, but I wanted him to hurry.

"You are breathtaking." Corbin closed the door to the bedroom behind him. He wrapped his arms around me and gently kissed my lips. I wished that somehow I could make everyone in the other room go away.

"You're not too bad yourself." I wiggled out of his arms and sat down in a chair. The bed was way too big of a temptation for a girl who had some confessing to do. "Come sit down. I've got to talk to you."

His face turned white. I knew he feared the worst.

I reached across the round table to hold his hand, like he'd done in his kitchen just a week before. It seemed like a lifetime ago. My mind teeter tottered over which piece of news to tell him first. If I told him about Westward, he might storm out of there to confront her without hearing about Shay. If I told him about Shay, he might storm out on me.

"I've got to tell you a couple of things, but you need to promise me that you won't leave until I'm done."

He let go of my hand, reassuring me with the caress of my cheek. "Dottie, I'm never going to leave you, no matter what it is."

I took in a deep, feeling the oxygen enter my lungs before blowing it out again. "Westward's stealing from the school. Percy's signing checks over to her. I saw her stash the night we had the meeting in her hotel room. That's how she was going to pay for this party, but I paid for it instead."

Corbin stared at me. I don't think he expected this news. "But that's impossible. She has to run her budget by us at every board meeting. We'd ask her what she was spending that money on." His eyes glossed over as his mind went into overdrive. "And ... Percy wouldn't do that."

"If she got him drunk enough, she could fool him. Is there any other fund that doesn't get run by you? A discretionary fund?"

"No, she has to run every little dime past us. If the books don't turn out right at the end of the school year, she's to blame and could go to prison." Corbin's mind was turning everything over right in front of me. "Unless … "

"Unless what?" I was on the edge of my seat. I wanted to nail the witch.

Corbin pulled out his cell phone and scanned through his phone list. "Let me call Bud and ask him a couple of questions."

I listened to Corbin's end of the conversation with the school board president.

After five minutes, he hung up and slammed his fist on the table. "We think she might be taking it from the Parent/Teacher Organization fund. Cheryl Johnson is the PTO president. Bud's going to call her and have her check on the funds. I know they had about thirty thousand dollars saved up for the new playground equipment. Maybe she wrote the checks before she left for Vegas."

I nodded. "She's also hobnobbing out there with other superintendents. I think she's looking for an escape."

Corbin turned his cell phone over and over in his hand, still shocked that the witch would steal from children. "So, you've known this since Thursday night. Why didn't you tell me? We could've moved on her sooner."

"That's the other thing I need to talk to you about." I was unsure if I could get the words out. I put my hand on top of his cell phone to keep him from spinning it. He looked up, letting me know that I had his attention.

"When I left, I said something to hurt you. Your kiss with Wanda Jo became a reality for me. It changed how I felt about Quandary, about my job, and about you. I didn't want anything to do with Quandary. I was running away. And along the way I met Shay."

"You don't have to tell me this." Corbin kept his eyes on mine. "We weren't together. You were angry."

"I don't want anything clouding our relationship." A tear rolled down my cheek. Corbin reached up and brushed it away, like he was trying to do with my relationship with Shay.

"He was so different from you, just like Vegas was so different from Quandary. But he refused to be a one-night stand, which was what I wanted. He wanted more from me than I had to give because any way I looked at it, the feelings I had for him were just a watered-down version of the feelings I have for you."

"So you didn't sleep with him." It was more of a statement then a question. Unfortunately, it had to be answered.

"The night before we got to Vegas, we'd been out drinking and I wish I could say that it didn't mean anything, but it did. But I've told him it's over."

Corbin got up and leaned his hands against the windowsill falsely enraptured by the lights below. "I love you, Dot. I don't want games, I just want you."

A few more tears fell as I put my arms around his waist from behind. I rested my head against his back. "Take me home, Corb. I'm not going to chase unknown rainbows anymore."

After discussing our Westward strategy, we headed back to the party. Our plan was to have Corbin talk individually to the superintendents that were so enraptured by Westward. I was going to play dumb and continue to serve food to the increasing masses. Oswald stood on the other side of the room, engaged in conversation with Ms. Nelson from the Las Vegas school district. When he saw me, he pardoned himself and headed my way.

"Can I have a word with you, Dottie?" Oswald led me into the entrance hallway. Once we were out of earshot, he continued, "I have an emerald in my apartment that's worth more than a quarter of the assets of this casino."

"Why are you telling me this?" It seemed an odd topic for hushed party conversation.

A young couple walked by. Oswald waited for them to pass before continuing. "It turned up missing the other night and I have reason to suspect Ms. Westward."

"Shocker," I mumbled. "What makes you suspect her?"

"I have a surveillance camera in my apartment and she's the one who took it."

"Why don't you just have her arrested? It sounds like you have the evidence." My mood continued to lift.

"I'd like to have the hard evidence. I have a team searching her hotel room as we speak. If you see anything suspicious, please let me know."

Westward came toward us. "Mr. Oswald! I've been looking all over for you. Tell me you've had some of the punch." She linked Oswald's elbow and dragged him back into the living area, so I went to refresh drinks.

At half past eight, a commotion near the doorway echoed through the room. Wearing children's masks to conceal their identities, three people burst into the party area. They were dressed all in black. The masks depicting the Scarecrow, the Tin Man, and the Lion came from the Emerald City gift shop on the first floor. The Scarecrow had a gun.

The partygoers screamed, some of them ducking behind the counter in the kitchen. I held a hot bucket of soapy water that I planned to use on the carpet where a particularly loaded principal spilled his red wine.

"Nobody move!" the gunman yelled. He marched over to me and held the gun to my head.

Corbin inched along the wall toward a heavy antique vase.

The short Tin Man grabbed the vase first and smashed it on the floor. "Don't even think of doing anything stupid."

The gunman, still holding the gun to my head, whispered in my ear. "You must be in the wrong place. The Miss Universe pageant is down in the ballroom." Leave it to Shay to use a lame pickup line in the middle of a fake hostage situation.

Shay yelled again. "I don't want to mess up this pretty girl's face with a bullet hole, so don't even think about calling the police."

Westward stepped forward, refusing to let three losers in black costumes mess up her party. "Go ahead."

"Step back, lady." Shay snarled through the mouth hole on the mask. "Or I'll shoot her brains out all over your plushy furniture."

"If you only had a brain, Scarecrow, you'd realize I don't care what you do to her." Westward was not willing to back down. "We'll get someone to clean it up."

"You'd let someone shoot me, Maxine?" I was amazed at her audacity.

"Why do I care? You're replaceable. Teachers are a dime a dozen." Westward now stood right in front of the ice sculpture. "The only ones that really matter are the movers in society—the ones who know how to get things done. You're going to be stuck in Quandary your whole life. Tramps like you don't matter."

"So stealing money from children is the way to be a mover in society?" I ripped my arm away from Shay. He spun around to point the gun at a couple of men sneaking up on him from behind.

Mr. Cucharas shook his head. He tore up the contract he'd prepared for Westward, her face turning red as he did.

"So you're not only a slut, you're a liar." There was spit flying out of her mouth with her words.

"Come on, Maxine. Didn't you learn about sticks and stones when you were in elementary school? Can't you be a little more original?" I placed the bucket on the floor beside me, no longer in danger of being shot, no longer in danger of slander. The one person in the room that mattered to me knew the truth.

Corbin finally dared to speak. "I put a call into Bud, Maxine. He did a little research and discovered money missing from the PTO funds. Oh, and Dottie and I have the whole slut issue worked out, so please cut the blackmail crap."

Shay lazily pointed the gun at Westward from behind as he made himself a plate from the silver serving dishes next to the ice sculpture. The fire from one of the burners suddenly caught on his sleeve and burst into flames. Without a second thought, I picked up the bucket and threw the water towards him, dousing Westward in the process. Shay and Westward were soaking wet.

"You brat!" Westward screeched after she wiped the water off her face. She clutched her body when she realized her white cotton dress was suddenly see through, but it wasn't her sagging breasts that people were looking at. Taped to her body were checks, hundred-dollar bills, and right on the small of her back was a large green bulge.

At that moment, Oswald nodded. Four police officers burst through the door.

"The strippers are here!" Tina squealed as Zeke pulled her toward the bedroom. Oswald rounded up Shay, Corbin, and me, and corralled us into the bedroom.

"The perpetrator is right there!" Oswald pointed his finger toward Westward. The three masked gunmen removed their masks in front of Corbin, who finally caught on to the charade. Oswald pushed my bed to the side. "Shay, come give me a hand."

Under my bed was a trap door. Where did that come from? "You never told me about that."

"Many of my loyal customers often need a quick escape, so I provide it for them." Oswald lifted the door in the carpeting. "This will take you down to the laundry room where there's an exit to the back of the building. I'll try to keep the focus on Ms. Westward and off of you."

When we got to the laundry, Corbin and I exited into the casino, unafraid to walk in public. His nose wrinkled at the bridge like it always did when he was angry. "Did you know about this?"

"Dear, right now is not the time to explain." I took his hand and pulled him to the elevator. We arrived at Corbin's door in no time at all.

The one suit Corbin owned hung in the closet beside his complimentary bathrobe. I unhooked it, and then began to search his drawers for his button-up shirt and tie.

"Dottie, are you going to tell me what's going on?" He leaned against the door watching me lay out his clothes like a mother.

"We were trapped at Westward's party. Shay, Zeke, and Tina came to rescue us. End of story." Pulling out his tie, I smiled. It was my favorite one with the light blue rhombuses that matched his eyes. "Now are you going to put your clothes on, or do I have to dress you, too?"

Chapter 20

"Did I mention how beautiful you look?" Corbin worked to knot his tie in front of the mirror. From behind, I stood on my tiptoes to help tie it properly into a Windsor knot. Being a country boy, Uncle Embry always needed help with the civilized stuff, for when he was forced to attend a funeral or a wedding.

"Yes, but a girl who can't take a compliment doesn't really care for the one dishing it out." I rested my chin on his shoulder, reaching on the balls of my feet.

"So, do you accept my compliment?" Corbin adjusted the cuffs on his jacket, which I found endearing because I didn't know how he could look any better.

"Haven't I always?" I flashed his reflection my best flirtatious smile before he turned around, lifted me up and threw me on the bed.

Removing the suit coat that he'd meticulously straightened moments before, he leaned so dangerously close to my face that I could smell the mint from his toothpaste, the scent of his cologne. Corbin bent over, kissing my neck. "No, you've never taken a compliment from me before."

"I'm sorry." I pulled him down closer to kiss his lips.

He lifted himself up to look me in the eyes again, the same eyes I'd been lost in many times before.

I ran my finger next to his eye and down his cheek. "I've treated you like some kind of personal joke for the past seven years. I wasn't going to get back together with you after I thought you cheated on me, but I know it was mean to flirt."

Corbin shook his head. "You haven't changed since the first day I met you, and I knew what I was getting myself into when I stayed around Quandary. You are the reason I stayed." He pressed his lips to mine, giving me a soft kiss. "And you're the only reason I'll leave."

~⌇~

The beat of loud music pounded through the hallway that led to the grand ballroom. Corbin and I weaved our way through teachers adorned in party garb. The party planners decorated the room to resemble a high school prom, complete with streamers and a green and gold balloon arch to greet us at the doorway. A banner stretching over one of the walls read, "Welcome to the Emerald City High School Prom!" The sheer tackiness of the whole event was exhilarating.

"How kind of them to recreate the scene of our last date." Corbin squeezed my hand. His words cut through me, and what he found funny, I found life changing.

"This is our chance to start over." I handed the man at the door our tickets. "It's like those couples you see on talk shows who've been separated for years, and then find each other again when they're eighty years old and on their death beds."

Corbin shook his head, keeping his comment to himself.

Making our way across the room, we found Tina and Zeke slow dancing in the middle of the action. Tina wore a bright blue dress covered with sequins and Zeke had on the same suit he wore to the salon.

"Can I have this dance?" Corbin held his hand out to me. Even when I had more respect for the stray dog that liked to pee in Aunt Henrietta's garden, I had to admit that Corbin had always been a gentleman.

When the music changed, Zeke tapped on Corbin's shoulder, cutting in before the start of the next song.

"So, the Tin Woman and the Lion are together at last." I turned my head to watch Corbin dance with Tina. He twirled her around and she giggled like a little girl dancing with her daddy.

"And it looks like Dottie Gale from Kansas has found her Prince Charming." Zeke squeezed my shoulders. "I haven't seen you take your eyes off of him since we were at that party. You got it bad, girl."

I gave Zeke a playful punch in the arm before he twirled me around—which wasn't so easy in my ruby high heels.

"Thanks, Dot, I'm a changed man and I owe it to you and Ozzie. I'd still be hiding behind my mama's skirt if it weren't for the two of you."

"Hey, what about me?" Tina caught the tail end of our conversation. Corbin stood in the drink line across the room. "You'd still be dressing up like Mace Windu if it weren't for me. Oh, wait a minute, you did dress up like him last night."

The old Zeke would've blushed and ran away, but instead he took Tina's hand. "Wait until you see Darth Vader tonight. He's been looking for his Padame."

"Alright." I suddenly felt very nauseous. "Remember to be ready at six tomorrow for our flight home."

"We've decided to stay here a little longer." Zeke smiled at Tina. "We might even take a bus back to Flagstaff."

"Wow, Zeke." I raised my eyebrows at him. "Do you realize that buses are breeding grounds for germs?"

"I told you that I'm a new man." Zeke pointed to his chest with his thumbs. "There's no going back."

"So, it looks like I'm flying solo with Oswald. I'm pretty sure Shay is going to stay here."

Tina scanned the room. "Speaking of Shay, we need to find him and his mystery date."

The line at the drink table zigzagged between three circular tables where people sat downing the red punch. We met Corbin near the middle of the line.

"Must be spiked. Free alcohol always draws a crowd like honey draws the flies. It's just easier to get rid of the flies in the bar."

Shay lounged at one of the tables, a plastic beer cup in his hand. He wore his jeans with the hole in the knee, a button down long-sleeve shirt with the top three buttons undone, and his cowboy hat. Three women leaned toward him at the table, hanging on his every word. His sex appeal and charisma lured girls in as much as any alcohol or honey. Before today, I'd been one of those women, captivated by this man with no inhibitions. When he saw me, he smiled, causing his flies to scatter, except for one.

"Dottie! Corbin! You guys look great! Come sit down and have a drink."

The pitcher of red punch on the table appeared low, but a waiter showed up and replaced it with a full one. Our table was the only one with a pitcher, so I wondered if it was some kind of VIP deal. The girl sitting next to Shay had long dark hair and striking green eyes, emphasized by her flawless make-up. If she were tall enough, she could easily model with the best of them.

While we sat down, Shay poured us each a plastic cup of the red mystery drink. "This is Courtney Oswald. She's in charge of the gallery that's opening downstairs in a couple of months."

A rich hotel owner's daughter. I'd seen more of them on reality shows then I cared to. Believe me. They walk around thinking they can buy anything and anyone, oblivious to the fact that we all couldn't care less. I'd rather hang out down at the homeless shelter in Quandary scooping shepherd's pie onto trays day in and day out than spend one minute with a stuck-up snob.

"So you're the great and powerful Oz's daughter." I grumbled, swishing the juice around in my cup to see if I could accidently stain the pristine tablecloth.

The jerk held out her hand to shake mine. "Yes, but I prefer Courtney. And you must be the famous Dottie Gale. My dad's told me all about you and how he's going to take you home tomorrow."

That's exactly how these girls operate. Reminding you of some kindness they, or in this case someone they knew, was providing for you with a miniscule fraction of their money and then making you feel indebted forever.

"What happened to the Jeep?" I guess I left out that minor detail with Corbin earlier today.

"It's dead. They're holding the funeral tomorrow at some junkyard in the suburbs. I guess I forgot to invite you."

"I would've bought you a plane ticket," Corbin said.

Shay took Courtney's hand and they made for the dance floor, not ready to be part of our first fight in seven years.

"That's just it. I didn't want to have to come to you to rescue me."

Corbin had his elbows on his knees, looking down at the floor. He'd taken on the role of my caretaker for half of his life. He sheltered me from bullying, carried my books when I broke my leg, attended every important event in my life. Sometimes I wondered if he dated me in high school to keep the other boys away from me, so they couldn't break my heart.

Corbin turned his head in my direction and I swear I saw a glint of liquid in his eyes. He sat up and took my hands in his. "I know I have to give up this obsession I have with protecting you, but I'd wish you let me take care of you once in a while."

"Tell you what." I stood up to sit on his lap, wrapping my arms around his neck. "After this wild and crazy prom, my feet are going to be killing me from these heels. I'm going to need someone to rub them."

"I think I can handle that." Corbin's eyes lit up again.

Shay and Courtney returned with some type of party platter filled with sandwiches and strawberries. Corbin left to use the restroom.

"Tell me more about the art gallery." I directed the question to both of them. Courtney and Shay seemed to come as a pair, so engaging in conversation with just one of them would be just plain rude, even for a country girl.

"All of the paintings will be African-inspired, but a lot of them will come directly from African artists. A large portion of the proceeds will go to help fight hunger on the continent." Courtney seemed excited about the exhibit.

"And the amazing thing," Shay continued. "Is this was all Courtney's idea. She loves art, modern art in particular, so she wanted to do something with that love. She's already been on three trips to different countries in Africa to assess the needs."

The room suddenly became very small and I wanted to apologize to Courtney for my unspoken judgments against her, but the DJ interrupted. "The next song goes out to Dottie Gale with love from Corbin."

The first beats of *Africa* by Toto began to fill the room, and the irony did not escape me. Shay grabbed Courtney again to head to the dance floor, leaving their half-eaten sandwiches behind. I looked around for Corbin. A light shone in the middle of the dance floor, which was way too obvious for a girl who's watched too many chick flicks.

He stood there holding a single red rose.

"I never thought about the words of this song before." Corbin smiled. We were dancing in the center of attention. I desperately tried to block the bride and groom vision from my head. "Where I'm at in my life right now, it would take a lot to take me away from you. I love you and want to spend every day of my life with you."

"I love you." I said, perfectly content in his arms.

⁓ ⌣ ⌣ ⌐

The cyclone that was Westward's disastrous party had miraculously disappeared when Corbin and I entered the suite after the dance. In its place were at least a hundred candles, strategically placed throughout the room, which I'm sure broke some kind of fire code. A sultry jazz singer filled the surround sound, singing of a love she'd lost and found again. A trail of rose petals meandered into the bedroom, stopping at the bed, and then branching off into the bathroom. The tub was steaming, full of suds and rose petals, making my feet ache in anticipation of a long soak.

"Did you?" I turned to Corbin, but his eyes told me that he was just as perplexed. Back in the living room, an envelope was propped up on the kitchen counter with my name on it.

Dottie,

> *I hope you don't mind that I sent housekeeping in to make a few improvements. I thought you and Corbin deserved something special. I will see you in the morning at 6:00 a.m. sharp.*

Nicholas Oswald

"Oswald did this for us." I put the card back down on the counter. Looking at Corbin, I knew there'd be no praying to the porcelain god tonight. "I think I'm ready for you to take care of me."

Chapter 21

Many people believe in fate, or an inevitable course in the universe. Imagine your life as a movie that you've never seen before on Netflix. It's all written, the actors chosen, the action scenes shot, and the climactic, or anti-climactic ending predestined. You can't watch the movie because you didn't pay your bill, but it's all there waiting, ready to play out in ninety minutes, or in some cases, ninety years.

When the crappy hotel alarm clock didn't go off at five o'clock the next morning, I was dreaming of my night with Corbin, his arm still draped over me. When the impatient taxi drivers out on Las Vegas Boulevard honked their horns at five-thirty under the gun to get their patrons to early flights at the airport, I rolled over and scrunched the pillow over my head. When the phone rang at five fifty-nine, my heart felt like it might jump out of my chest and I wondered if it was a snow day. When Corbin sat up beside me, I recalled almost all the important details.

"Hello?" I had on my groggy, morning voice.

"I know I'm calling a little late and you're probably heading out the door, but I wanted to say good-bye." The most important detail swam back into my head as my eyes glanced at the clock. I almost hung up the phone on Shay.

"Crap, Shay! I've got to go!" I threw the phone back down in the base before running around the room like a madwoman. Corbin worked on my suitcase while I got dressed and ran a brush through my hair.

One hand was brushing my teeth while the other was applying mascara when Corbin came up from behind. "I'll carry your suitcase down and try to catch Oswald. Don't worry if you forget anything, my flight isn't until two, so I'll check the room well."

After spitting, I rinsed my mouth and then turned around to give Corbin a kiss for being the best boyfriend in the world. "I love you, babe. Can't wait to see you tonight."

"It's a date," Corbin said, and then left the room to find Oswald.

～ ～

When I reached the lobby with my carry-on, Corbin was sitting with my suitcase near the fountain. He came over when he saw me. "Oswald's gone."

"What do you mean, he's gone?"

"He left without you. I asked his bodyguard over there. He had to leave at six to make it to his meeting on time in Oklahoma." Corbin grinned. "I guess I'll just have to buy you a ticket to fly home with me."

"No, you're not buying me a ticket." I wasn't quite sure why I needed to be so independent, especially after my conversation with Corbin last night. "I'm going to make a phone call. How about I meet you for breakfast in an hour."

"I'm sorry." He bent over to kiss my forehead. "I should've thought to set the alarm."

Heading to the elevator, I gave my red mustang a love tap, wishing I could leave this place in style instead of having to grovel. The entire way up the elevator, I tried to convince myself to swallow my pride and let Corbin do something for me, but I was still highly unconvinced. The idea of a man giving me money was a lot harder to take than a woman lending it to me, so when I reached the suite, I picked up the phone to call Wanda Jo.

"Hello?" Wanda answered the phone quicker than I expected.

"Hey, Wanda. It's me, Dottie."

"Why haven't you called me? I've been sitting here on the edge of my seat wondering if my matchmaking worked." I could feel Wanda Jo's pout through the phone.

"Um, it's been busy."

"So tell me everything. Are you back together? Did he love your dress? Did you sleep with him?"

"Yes, yes, and I don't kiss and tell." It was like I was checking off a list. "But that's not why I called."

"What do you mean that's not why you called? Of course that's why you called. Why else do girls talk unless it's to talk about clothes or guys?"

"To ask for favors." I inflected my voice slightly at the end in hopes of sounding desperate.

"What do you need, honey?"

"To borrow some money to get home."

"What happened to your car?"

"It died. Don't talk about it too much. I'm still getting over it."

"I'm sure Corbin's offered," Wanda started. "Wait a minute. Don't tell me he's being a cheapskate, because I see what he brings in on the weekends."

"No, it's not him. It's me. I can't ask him. I've treated him so bad that I already have seven years to make up for. I don't want to owe him money, too."

"You're being silly. But of course you can borrow it. How much do you need?"

"About two hundred. I have fifty left over from my poker winnings."

"Why don't you sell the ruby slippers? That way you'll get the money faster."

"But aren't they a family heirloom or something?"

"Nah." Wanda laughed. "Just a gift from some rich boyfriend a few years back. He says the stones are real rubies, so you should be able to get a good price for them."

"Thanks, Wanda. I don't know what I'd do without you."

"You'd have to hang out with Saundie and talk about standardized testing and the newest Westward rumors. She's been fired by the way. The criminal hearing is going to start in November. Maybe you need to become a private investigator."

"It's called snooping, Wanda. Not that difficult."

"Yeah, but you stuck your neck out for the school. Uncle Percy said they're going to put up some plaque in your name and present it at the next board meeting." She sounded proud, like she was best friends with a real hero. "He feels terrible about letting Westward pull one over on him. He's quit drinking and is attending AA."

"That's great, Wanda." I wondered what kind of rumors Miggy had already started about how everything went down. She probably had Westward and me mud wrestling over the bag of money.

After getting dressed, I placed the ruby heels into my oversized purse and went down to the coffee shop.

Corbin already had breakfast waiting with a steaming cup of coffee that I was eternally grateful for. Although he hinted at my phone call, trying to unravel the secret of my plan, I kept the shoes hidden. He left disappointed, and uninformed, to pack up his room while I walked toward the revolving door. Shay was coming in as I was heading out.

"You're still here." Shay scratched his head. He wore a suit, blue and pinstriped. Shiny black shoes stuck out from the bottom of his pant legs; his hair was pulled back in a tie.

"Yep, missed the plane." I was still taking in his new look. "Did anyone tell you that … "

"I look great?" Shay blushed, a phenomenon I had never seen before. "Yeah, I think a few people have."

"No, that you forgot your cowboy hat." I tried not to lay the flirt on too thick. "Do you want to go for a walk?"

"Sure. I've got a meeting at one. Don't you have a plane you have to catch?"

"Not yet." We passed through the entryway with its grand pillars and ornate detailing, ready to impress the incoming guests. Three valet drivers stood around waiting for their next tip, overdressed in the eighty-degree temperatures. "I have to pay for a flight before I can make a flight."

"Do you need to borrow … " Shay started.

"No."

"Forget I asked." Shay pouted. We walked in silence for a couple of blocks past a wonderland of sensory overload. "Doesn't this place remind you of Disneyworld? You know, except for the billboards of half-naked women. Instead of handing out candy on Main Street, they hand out flyers advertising for sex."

I stopped mid-step and threw my arms around Shay. He stood stiff for a moment, but then relaxed into my hug. I squeezed him tight. "I'm going to miss you more than anyone I've ever missed before."

"I'll miss you too." People flowed around us like we were a boulder in the middle of a river. "Come back and see my exhibit when it opens next summer."

"You know I wouldn't miss it." I looked up at him. I'd made my choice, and it was good to have him as a friend.

"So where are we going?" Shay took my arm. "A little last minute souvenir shopping?" He picked up a snow globe with Elvis swinging his hips inside and shook it so the snow looked like dandruff in the King's black locks. "Because I know you need one of these."

I put the globe back on the shelf, grabbed his hand, and kept him moving.

The pawnshop was located on a side street off Las Vegas Boulevard, between a strip joint and a vacant lot. The black bars across the windows reminded me of Zeke's place in Flagstaff—very welcoming. A flashing silver light spun around and around, indicating the shop was open despite the lack of patrons. The bell above the door alerted the clerk to our arrival, but the pimply-faced kid behind the counter continued to lounge on his stool, thumbing through a magazine.

When we approached the cash register, he lifted his eyes from his reading material. "Got something to sell?" The kid stood up and rested his hands on the glass display case. He couldn't have been more than nineteen, stuck in a pawnshop instead of off to college. Las Vegas had as many dead ends as the rest of America. It just shoved them in the black corners away from the flashy lights.

Placing my bag on the counter, I pulled out the heels. He picked them up to examine their condition, but spent most of the time looking at the stones on the front. "They real?"

"Of course they're real." I acted put off that he'd ask such a question.

He grunted. "I'm going to have Kurt look at the rubies. I'll bring them right back." He took the shoes, and disappeared through a curtain in the back of the store.

Kurt must've been pretty busy because it took the kid at least twenty minutes to return. No one came in, so Shay and I wandered the store perusing, the hundreds of items that people found less valuable than money.

"I can give you two hundred, but that's the best I can do." The kid looked like he was bracing himself for an argument.

"I'll take it." I knew the kid was getting a deal.

<hr/>

A tour bus pulled up to the front entrance of the Emerald City at the same time Shay and I returned. The valet station became senior citizen central, so we waited to let them enter the hotel's lobby. One older lady with a cane placed her hand on my arm and turned to the man I assumed was her husband, "Look at the young lovers, George. You used to be that handsome in pinstripes." She ran her hand down the arm of Shay's suit. "George and I have been married for sixty-five years. We've taken a honeymoon each one of those years. Keep up the romance and the spontaneity, and you two will last that long." Older people always felt the need to give advice to me, even under erroneous assumptions.

"The sex helps, too." George winked at Shay.

"You've got that right, Georgie." Shay gave George a playful punch in the arm before I grabbed his arm and dragged him into the casino.

"I'll help you pack." We weaved through the slot machines. "I've got a few more hours."

"It's already done." I stopped beside the mustang and dug out a five from my ruby slipper profits. "Corbin was just going to check the room to see if I left anything behind."

Sitting in front of the slot machine, absently pulling the handle, I thought about my little house back in Kansas and sleeping in my own bed.

Shay stood beside me. "You realize they rig these machines so it's near impossible to win."

"Just five bucks." I pulled the handle again. "It's going to Oswald. He gave me a free suite, the least I could do is give him five dollars."

Shay wandered down the row of empty machines, feeding a dollar bill into one of them while throwing his lopsided grin at me. A bell at my own machine drew my attention away from him. Three bright red convertibles lined up perfectly on the centerline of the screen and a light flashed on the top of the machine. My hands began to shake and I jumped up and ran over to Shay. "I won! The mustang's mine! The ruby slippers are bringing me home!"

A crowd of people gathered around us, trying to catch a glimpse of the woman who won the car. A photographer and a man with a microphone pushed their way through the crowd. "Congratulations!" The announcer crooned. "The Emerald City Casino is the home to more winners than any other casino on the strip!"

The photographer snapped several pictures of me sitting on the stool. Then he had me stand up and have my picture taken with Shay.

"What's your name?" The man held the microphone up to my mouth.

"Dottie Gale." I was still beaming from ear to ear. My heart raced out of control, and I suddenly giggled thinking about driving a mustang on my pothole ridden driveway.

The man spoke through the microphone again. "The casino would like to congratulate Dottie Gale, the grand prize winner of the Ford Mustang convertible."

Corbin stood at the front of the crowd, his eyes on me, a simple smile on his lips.

Chapter 22

"So this was your grand plan?" Corbin asked when we finally had a moment alone. "Luck? I'd say we should go to Vegas, but ... "

"My plan was to borrow money from Wanda Jo." I looked down at the paperwork, filling in my home address. "She let me sell the ruby heels."

"I'm just going to swallow my manly pride and pretend I understand why you could borrow money from Wanda and not from me." Corbin straightened out the stack of papers I already filled out, tapping them on the edge on the table.

"Well, you just go ahead and do that." I signed my name to the bottom of another paper. "You should know what you're getting into. I've been this way all my life." I stopped writing for a moment and looked at him. "And while we're at it, there are a couple of things I want to ask you."

"What's that, dear?" Corbin tilted his head.

"Will you drive home with me? There's a dead mouse behind a billboard in New Mexico I need to dig up." The ring couldn't have sustained that much damage after being under the ground for less than a week.

Corbin shifted slightly in his seat at my comment, but answered, "Of course I'll drive home with you and help you find your ... dead mouse."

I searched for a way to approach the next subject with a man as prideful as I was stubborn. "I've been thinking that I'd like to get a roommate to help me out with the bills. Do you know anybody looking for a place to stay?"

Corbin sucked in his breath. "I think I know someone. He wants to rent out his apartment to his high school buddy. Says it's too small." Corbin appeared nervous, like he always did before a championship game in high school. "There'd need to be some kind of written contract, or he'd never concede."

"Your friend drives a tough bargain." I wasn't sure where Corbin was heading.

He stood up, took hold of my hands, and pushed his chair aside with his foot. While he was getting down on one knee, the casino representative opened the door, but then did a one-eighty and went immediately out again.

"Dottie Gale, I'm tired of playing it safe. I'm tired of hiding my feelings for you. I love you and I'm willing to let the world know how I feel."

"I love you, Corbin." Although he was my best friend, my hands still shook.

"Will you marry me, Dorothy Marie Gale?" His eyes held mine with a fierceness that I'd never seen before from his blue lakes of calm. "I can't live another day pretending that I'm your boss and that you don't matter to me."

"But you are my boss, Mr. Lane." I tried to suppress the nervousness in my voice with humor. My head swam with images from the dream with the rock on my finger, but Shay never entered into it. Instead, Corbin was the one making love to me after his shower.

"Then, I've officially resigned today. I'll call Bud the first chance I get." He let go of one of my hands and cupped the side of my face.

"Yes." I no longer bothered to hide the tears. "Yes, I'll marry you."

"Let's do it today." Excitement filled his eyes in a new and unfamiliar way. "There's a little chapel around the corner."

"I think there's a chapel on every corner." I wiped the tears with my sleeve. "We don't need to rush. I know you'd want the church, and the dress, and the whole shebang."

"Then let's make it our secret. I don't look that great in a dress anyways." He gave me a lopsided grin. "We'll do it up back in Quandary, but let's not wait any longer. I'll call the school and get you a substitute for a few more days."

There comes a point in every girl's life when she needs to decide if she's going to spend her life with a Shay or a Corbin. There are other names and personality types to throw into the mix like Biff, but I'm sure you catch my drift here. It was in this conversation that I became aware of Corbin's desire to sprinkle a little more Shay into his lifestyle. I rewarded his courage by agreeing to his crazy idea.

Shay, Tina, and Zeke agreed to be our witnesses, along with Adele and George, the elderly couple I met earlier in the day. They seemed a little confused when they found out that Corbin was the groom instead of Shay, but they just assumed it was part of the *free love* practiced nowadays. I wore a yellow summer dress, since it was the closest I had to white, and carried a bouquet of daisies. Corbin wore the suit he had on last night at the dance. He arranged for the singing Elvis to perform *Africa*. It felt appropriate to include Toto in our wedding since it had now become our song. Believe me, it is something I'll never forget.

And Corbin, he looked amazing. I don't know if it was the daylight, or his newfound ability to do something spontaneous that made him look so perfect. When the Justice of the Peace prompted him, he pulled out the most beautiful diamond ring. "I bought it five years ago. I knew then. I've always known, Dottie."

I couldn't respond as the tears filled my eyes. I simply held my hand to my mouth, unable to find words as perfect as the ones passing over his lips.

Tina and Zeke decorated the mustang with the usual honeymoon trimmings. Shaving cream letters spelled out *Quandary or Bust* on the back window of the car. I looked at Tina and winked.

"Thank you for taking a chance on a hitch-hiker like me." Tina hugged me. "And thanks for getting me out of jail. I'm sorry I caused you so much trouble."

I pulled out of her embrace. "You weren't …"

"Dottie Gale! Whoops, I mean, Dottie Lane!" Tina threw her hands to her hips like a scolding mother. "You know I was more trouble than a second grader in the principal's office."

"Well, you did make things interesting." I placed my hand on her arm. "But I wouldn't have wanted things any different."

"Me either." Zeke cut in front of Tina to give me a hug. "I'm going to help Tina work it out with the courts to get Gracie and Canton to come stay with us over Christmas break in Flagstaff. She's going to get a job in the school that I work in and prove that she's fit to get her children back."

"That's great, Tina." I knew how much she really loved her children. "Keep in touch. I want to know what happens."

"You know I will." The couple walked off to make a dinner reservation at the Paris hotel.

Shay came over and shook Corbin's hand. "If you were any less of a man, I'd have to beat you senseless, but I can see how happy you make her."

Corbin squeezed my hand and got into the driver's seat of the car, trying to give the two of us some space to say good-bye.

"I guess this is it." I wrapped my arms around his neck.

"This is normally where I come in and say something highly intellectual and funny, but the words are escaping me." Shay kept his arms around my waist. "I'm really going to miss you, Dottie."

"I'll miss you, too." My heart ached saying goodbye to my new friend.

I pulled back and caught a tear rolling down his face before he quickly wiped it away.

"If he ever mistreats you, or you grow tired of Quandary or something. Well, you know where to find me." Shay scuffed the sole of his boot on the sidewalk, and I could tell he was fighting to hold back something that he really wanted to say.

"What are you going to tell Randy about your job?"

"That I've moved on. There's always a line of prospective teachers falling over each other to get a job in Amarillo. It won't be tough for him."

Corbin started the engine, ready to start our honeymoon, so I turned to get in the passenger side, but Shay grabbed my hand. "I know this is hardly the appropriate time to say this, but I love you, Dottie."

"I love you, Shay." I turned to look at Corbin in the car, patient as ever. "But not as much as I love that man in there." And with that, I opened the door and drove off to my happily ever after with Corbin.

So what have I learned in this adventure called life? Everyone kept telling me that they hoped I found what I was looking for along the way. And I did. I found myself. Exotic places like Las Vegas and Africa, where Corbin and I spent our second honeymoon, are interesting to visit, but nothing grounds a person as much as the place they grew up and the people they grew up with.

And with Westward gone, there really is no place like home.